The TICKING HEART

ANDREW KAUFMAN

COACH HOUSE BOOKS | TORONTO

first edition

Published with the generous assistance of the Canada Council for the Arts and the Ontario Arts Council. Coach House Books also acknowledges the support of the Government of Canada through the Canada Book Fund and the Government of Ontario through the Ontario Book Publishing Tax Credit.

Any resemblence to persons living or dead is purely coincidental.

LIBRARY AND ARCHIVES CANADA CATALOGUING IN PUBLICATION

Title: The ticking heart / Andrew Kaufman.
Names: Kaufman, Andrew, 1968- author.
Identifiers: Canadiana (print) 20190142987 | Canadiana (ebook) 20190143037 | ISBN 9781552453896 (softcover) | ISBN 9781770565845 (PDF) | ISBN 9781770565838 (EPUB)
Classification: LCC PS8571.A892 T53 2019 | DDC C813/.6—dc23

The Ticking Heart is available as an ebook: ISBN 978 1 77056 583 8

Purchase of the print version of this book entitles you to a free digital copy. To claim your ebook of this title, please email sales@chbooks.com with proof of purchase. (Coach House Books reserves the right to terminate the free digital download offer at any time.)

For Carl. My brother.

THE RETURN OF THE MAN
IN THE PURPLE HAT

Two hours and seventeen minutes into his forty-third year, Charlie Waterfield realized he was lost. He was standing at the corner of Euclid and Barton in downtown Toronto. He could have walked home if he'd wanted to. He probably should have. What prevented him from doing so was the painful realization that he was lost inside the one thing it is impossible to escape: his own life.

This was his second birthday since the separation, the first he'd spent on his own, and he really thought he'd be happy by now. His kids had made him dinner but they were spending the night with their mom. Wanda, the woman he was seeing and possibly in love with, had taken him to his favourite theatre and bought him drinks at his favourite bar. And yet all of these expressions of affection hadn't been enough to make him happy. And he knew that they should have been. He knew he was in no mood to share anything: not a bed, not secrets, and certainly not an Uber. So when the four-door sedan stopped in front him and Charlie saw that there was already someone in the back, he became angry.

Charlie checked his phone, which confirmed that the black Nissan Rouge was the car he'd requested and that he'd accidently hit 'Pool' when ordering it. Charlie looked over his shoulder, up at the window of Wanda's bedroom. The light on her bedside table was still on. He regretted not accepting her offer to spend the night.

When Charlie looked back at the Nissan, he couldn't help noticing that the man in the back seat wore a large hat. The most striking thing about it was its colour, an alarmingly bright purple that seemed to drift into the air like smoke. The brim was extremely wide, so large that he must have taken the hat off before climbing in and then made a conscious decision to put it back on. The hat's colour and size combined to create the impression of an entirely separate passenger, as if the back seat already held two people and Charlie would be the third.

This was not how Charlie Waterfield wanted to start his forty-third year. The idea that this car would take him to his apartment and not to the house he still considered home made him very sad. The wind was cold. He'd forgotten his gloves, and his hands were freezing. Shivering, Charlie opened the back door of the car: as it turns out, he was making one of the most important decisions of his life because he was cold and tired and just wanted to get to bed. Which is, of course, how all of life's most important decisions are made.

The man in the purple hat smiled broadly and shuffled to the left, making room for Charlie to sit down. As the car pulled away from the curb, Charlie couldn't stop looking at the hat, which the man under it interpreted as a desire to talk.

'Strange time to be going home.' The brim of his hat wobbled as he spoke, marking his speech like hand gestures.

'Hmmm?' Charlie, against his better judgment, continued staring at the hat.

'Most people, you'd have to assume, are already home or have decided to stay where they are. And here you are, trudging home at this ungodly hour on this cold night.'

'Yes.'

'Makes one wonder why.'

'Why what?' Charlie took care to overenunciate his words. He did this to compensate for the man in the purple hat's English accent, which made his own seem provincial.

'Why didn't you stay where you were?'

Charlie found the strength to look down at his knees. Several moments passed. Unable to resist the pull of the hat, Charlie looked back up at it. The man in the purple hat was still looking at him.

'Do you mind?' the man in the purple hat said as he pointed to Charlie's chest. It was at this moment that two very strange things happened. The first was that Charlie knew, without a doubt, that the man in the purple hat was suggesting that Charlie allow him to listen to his heart. The second was that Charlie knew, also without a doubt, that he was going to let him do it.

Charlie unbuttoned his jacket, although he kept the buttons on his shirt done up. The man pushed his purple hat toward the back of his head, so it sat above his forehead in a way that seemed to rebuke gravity. Lowering his head, he pressed his right ear flush against Charlie's chest.

'Do you hear that? Something slogging around in there. A hopeful sound. But you know, hope can be a very dangerous thing.'

'Slogging?'

'Thank you.' The man in the purple hat sat up and pulled his hat back into position. The movement drew

Charlie's attention. He discovered that, once again, he was unable to look away from it.

'Have you ever heard of a city named Metaphoria?' asked the man in the purple hat.

'No.'

'That's because it doesn't exist, at least not like this city or others like it do. The city of Metaphoria is like Brigadoon, or Avalon, or Echo Beach. It is the sort of place that most people think is a fiction, a fairy tale. Let me assure you, Metaphoria is no fiction. It is a very real place. A city with buildings and streets and citizens. But it is a city very few people ever get the opportunity to visit.'

Charlie immediately stopped staring at the purple hat and looked down at his knees again. He had determined the man in the purple hat to be off balance. Charlie shifted his body to the right, pointing his knees and torso as far away from the man in the purple hat as possible and looked out the window. This is when he saw the large white snowflakes falling from the sky. Charlie found it very difficult not to take the fact that it was snowing, in April, on his birthday, personally.

'Metaphoria is a place you simply appear. One moment you're living your life to the best of your abilities, and the next, poof, you find yourself on the streets of Metaphoria. What brought you there? It's simple: everyone there has something they can't get over: a belief or love or antiqued self-image. Perhaps a painful memory they can't stop defining themselves by.

'Does any of this sound familiar to you, Charlie?'

'Yes.' Charlie was surprised by the sound of his voice. He hadn't realized he was speaking until he heard it. He looked at the man in the purple hat, although his knees and torso continued to point at the door of the car.

'Metaphoria is a city that isn't based on realism. The organizing principle in Metaphoria is metaphor. It is a city specifically designed to trigger epiphanies. And that's a very important word to remember, Charlie. Epiphany! Because that's the only way out of Metaphoria. Six buses, four trains, and eighteen flights leave Metaphoria each and every day – but all of them arrive at the same bus depot, train station, or airport they departed from. There is only one way to leave Metaphoria, and that is to go out on the same puff of purple smoke and smell of cedar you came in on. In Metaphoria, this is known as a ... poof!'

'Poof?' For the first time Charlie looked the man in the eyes and not the hat.

'Poof!'

'Poof.'

'And the only way to trigger a poof is to have an epiphany. As a recently divorced man – wait, let me correct myself ... because that's the whole point of all of this, isn't it? Because you're not recently divorced, are you, Charlie? You haven't been a husband for two years? Yes? That's long enough to figure out that it isn't the bite that kills you but the venom.'

'Are we talking about snakes?'

'You're spending all this time and energy and effort resenting the snake for biting you. That's the last thing you should be doing. Charlie, you have spent seven hundred and thirty days focusing on the fact that you've been bitten and not on the venom coursing through your veins!'

'How did you know I was recently divorced?'

'Two years is not recent.'

'We were together for twenty years.'

'Living in Metaphoria gets tricky, though, because nobody has just one problem. Everyone has multiple problems. And Metaphoria manifests all of them. To be in Metaphoria is to see all your problems at once, manifested at the same time, like ivy at the height of summer.

'There will be times when all of Metaphoria seems dead set against you, Charlie. As if the entire city has been specifically constructed to poke you in the places you wish not to be poked. You just have to trust that it's all for your own good.'

Charlie turned his body to face the man in the purple hat. The man opened his eyes wider than Charlie thought possible and tipped the brim of his hat backward, causing it to rub against the roof of the car.

'Don't worry about panicking. Everybody panics.'

Charlie could smell burning cedar. He felt woozy. He rested his forearms on the tops of his legs. He looked down at the floor of the car. And then there was so much purple smoke that Charlie couldn't see anything else.

Poof!

THE EPIPHANY DETECTIVE AGENCY

For several moments Charlie couldn't see anything but purple smoke, and when it started to clear, Shirley Miller plunged a knife into his chest. The blade was serrated. The handle was pearl. She pushed it deeper. Using both hands and all of her strength, Shirley sawed downward. She cut through bone and muscle. This caused Charlie to scream, loudly. He didn't move his arms or legs or any other part of his body. He couldn't. The only part of Charlie that wasn't as wooden as the chair underneath him was his vocal cords. All he could do was scream as Shirley cut an eight-inch incision in his chest.

She pulled out the knife, flicking a drop of blood into the air. The drop hung motionless for a fraction of a second. It changed shape, from a drop to a heart, then it fell. The heart-shaped drop left a heart-shaped stain on the hardwood.

'This might hurt a bit, Charlie.'

Reaching through the incision, Shirley grabbed Charlie's heart. She tightened her grip and ripped Charlie's heart out of his chest. When she uncurled her fingers, Charlie's heart sat in the middle of Shirley's open palm. It was at this moment that Charlie began to panic. His panic was triggered not just by the fact that Shirley had stabbed him in the chest, or that his heart currently beat on her open palm, although these were contributing factors. What really panicked Charlie was that he recognized Shirley from university. They had dated for a year and half.

'Oh, Charlie. Did you never learn to take care of this thing?'

Charlie's heart did not look great. The pulmonary veins were swollen and purple. A long scar ran from the base of his aorta all the way across to the left ventricle. Smaller scars criss-crossed his right auricle. The superior vena cava leaned to the left at a strange angle. Although his heart beat in a steady rhythm, it seemed to do so with great reluctance. It had been years since Charlie had treated his heart with care and respect. This was because he had a long list of grievances about his heart. He didn't like that his heart made him so vulnerable. He didn't like how slow it was to heal. Even now, two years after he was legally divorced, Charlie's heart continued to gush out sadness early in the morning and late at night.

However, the thing Charlie disliked the most about his heart was that it could be so disloyal. He had not wanted to fall out of love with his wife. She had not wanted to fall out of love with him. And yet both of these things had happened, causing Charlie to spend his days hoping that the situation would change, that their love would return. The fact that it never did seemed like a betrayal to him. And now here it was falling in love with Wanda. Charlie had grown to believe his heart was not to be trusted.

He had spent the last two years, if not longer, living as if his heart weren't part of him. He had ignored everything his heart had suggested. He had not allowed it to contribute to any decisions he made. But as he watched his heart wearily beat on Shirley's open palm, Charlie's only desire was to get it back inside him.

'It's been a while since I've been this close to your heart,' she said.

'Although, if I remember correctly, this isn't the first time you ripped it out.'

As Charlie said this, his heart beat just a little bit faster. Shirley noticed, but she was kind enough not to mention it. She gave Charlie's heart a tender squeeze. She was one of those tall blond women with wide shoulders whose confidence and straight-ahead manner protect a sincere sentimentality. As she looked down at Charlie's heart, she found it certifiably ugly and in such an advanced state of disrepair she wondered if it could ever be fixed. However, she also saw something noble in its determination to continue beating, which caused her own heart to beat just a little bit stronger and a little bit faster. Her long fingers treated Charlie's heart with delicate care as she wrapped it in a blue linen cloth and put it into her purse.

Charlie could see his heart beating inside Shirley's purse. From that same purse, Shirley took out a bomb. The bomb looked homemade. Seven sticks of dynamite were duct-taped together and connected to a digital clock with a single green wire. Shirley pressed a red button and the bomb started ticking. She pushed the bomb through the incision in Charlie's chest. It sat right where Charlie's heart should have been. Taking a needle and a spool of fishing line from her purse, Shirley began stitching up Charlie's incision. She worked carefully. Her fingers made small, precise movements. She was trying to leave as small a scar as possible. It saddened Shirley to know that no matter how hard she tried or how carefully she worked, there would be a scar. Which, as we all know, is the way these things work.

'Your heart weighs much more than the bomb.'

'Does that mean something?'

'This is Metaphoria, Charlie. Everything means something. What are you carrying in there?'

'Sadness?'

'Sadness weighs less than that.'

'How do you know I'm carrying anything in there?'

'Everybody's carrying something in their heart. One of the few benefits of living in Metaphoria is that you finally get to see what it is.'

'What's in yours?'

'For me it's not what's in it so much as the size.'

'Your heart's too small?'

'It's too big, Charlie. My heart loves too much. This motivates me to do horrible things in order to keep that love. Case in point: what I've just done to you.'

Shirley tied a knot in the fishing line. Leaning close to his chest, she bit off the thread. It was at this moment that Charlie's panic returned. His eyes grew wide. His breathing turned rapid and, feeling dizzy, Charlie became convinced that he was going to pass out.

'It's okay. It's okay.'

'I'm just … It's…'

'Everybody panics when they arrive. Just breathe. Concentrate on breathing. Remember, there is a way home.'

'That's right. Right. I just … to get home … I have to have an epiphany?'

'You have to have a certain kind of epiphany. But you're right, that's how we get home.'

'There are different types of epiphanies?'

'It helps if you think about it in the form of a question.' Straddling his lap, Shirley put both of her hands on his face and looked into his eyes. 'Think of your epiphany as the answer to a question. Find that answer, trigger your epiphany, and there you go, poof, sailing home on the same gust of purple smoke and smell of burning cedar you came in on.'

'What's the question?'

'What's the purpose of the human heart?'

'It's not to push blood through the body?'

'Not around here.'

'To emote?'

'You're going to have to be more specific than that. Because the thing is, there isn't one answer to that question. That's why it's such a great question! Every citizen of Metaphoria has their own answer. The purpose of the human heart is different for everybody who has one. Answer that question, for real, for you, and you'll trigger your poof.'

Shirley looked down at her blouse and found a small red stain. This was one of her favourite shirts and she was angry at herself for having been so careless. She attempted to get rid of the stain using a handkerchief and spit. Her motions were vigorous. She forgot that Charlie was even in the room, much less that his heart was beating in her purse. Finally, she gave up trying to remove the stain, looked up, and was startled to see that she was still straddling his lap.

She looked around the room. Following her lead, Charlie did the same. He appeared to be in some sort of office, behind a wooden desk, sitting in a wooden chair. The office was neither luxurious nor busy.

'As far as arrivals go, Charlie, you've done pretty well for yourself. You have arrived in Metaphoria as the sole detective of the Epiphany Detective Agency. Why am I here? Well, I suspect that the metaphoric implications will soon be revealed to us. Presently, I am in need of your services.

'My husband has lost his heart. I need you to find it. I know you're dying to make a smart-ass comment. You want to ask me if I've checked his other pants. The glovebox? Next you'll want to suggest that maybe it's not lost – maybe someone stole it. Finally, a smug masculine superiority will beam out of you as you give me a look that implies you've thought of something I haven't. You'll pause dramatically before asking, "Isn't it possible that he simply gave it away to someone else?"'

This was true. Charlie wanted to do and say all of these things.

'So let's just forgo all of that. I'm his wife, Charlie. I feel its absence. I need it back. He can't love me without it. You can have your heart back when you bring me his. You have twenty-four hours.'

'And then?'

'Charlie goes boom.' She paused. 'My husband works in the Tachycardia Tower. He'll be easy to spot. His friends call him Twiggy.'

'That's all you're going to give me? A nickname and address?'

'And twenty-four hours. Don't forget that, Charlie. That's very important.'

'That isn't enough!'

'This is Metaphoria, Charlie. If that isn't more than ample, there's no hope for any of us.'

3

THE TWO CHANNELS

As Shirley closed the door to the Epiphany Detective Agency behind her, the office became quiet. Charlie could hear nothing but the ticking of the bomb in his chest. The sound was disconcerting because it hit his eardrums from inside. This was something Charlie had never experienced before. He did not like it. Feeling overwhelmed, he lifted his feet, put his hand on the corner of the desk, and pushed, which caused his chair to spin, something he hadn't done since he was a child.

Charlie watched the room revolve. The furniture included the desk he sat behind, two chairs in front of it, a bookshelf, and nothing else. The wall behind the desk had one small window. The wall across from the desk was covered with framed headshots of, Charlie assumed, all the other people who had worked as a detective in this office before him. The chair stopped spinning, allowing Charlie to see that the last picture in the bottom row was his.

He looked at his watch. The face no longer showed the time. It was now a digital countdown of how many seconds, minutes, and hours Charlie had before the bomb in his chest exploded.

His watch said:

23 HR 58 MIN 11 SEC

Charlie realized he had a literal expiry date. He looked away from the watch. He noticed a walkie-talkie, which was black, rectangular, and, because of its positon in the precise centre of the desk, impossible to ignore. It appeared to be an exact replica of the one he'd had when he was eleven. Charlie briefly wondered if it was the very same one, until he saw the modification. Where the walkie-talkie Charlie had when he was eleven featured a dial that let him choose from seven channels, this one had a switch, offering only two channels.

One was marked

LINDA (EX-WIFE)

The other read

WANDA (UNCOMMITTED LOVER)

Charlie resented both the 'ex' before 'wife,' and the 'uncommitted' before 'lover.' He wondered if either Linda or Wanda would have felt the same way. It did not take him long to decide they wouldn't. Charlie turned the walkie-talkie on. A green light in the upper right-hand corner shone, revealing that the device was fully charged. The switch that selected the channel sat in between the two options. Charlie had a decision to make. Quickly, he selected 'Linda.'

'Linda?'

'Charlie? Hello? Charlie?'

Her voice sounded like home. Not just any home, but the home Charlie longed to return to. A home where the divorce never happened, where the daily course of ordinary events, the raising of children, various professional promotions and setbacks, twenty years of pettiness and empathy fatigue hadn't caused them to inch farther apart, until reunification became an impossibility. Here in Metaphoria, it was clear to Charlie that this home was not a location, or even a belief, but a delusion, a vision manifested by wishful thinking and unrealistic hope. Charlie knew this to be true. That did not make him want to go there any less.

'Yes, I'm here. I'm here. How are you?'

'Don't forget that Friday's a P.A. day.' Charlie could hear his kids arguing in the background, the scrape of the chairs across the floor. This is how Charlie knew that while he was using a walkie-talkie, Linda believed she was simply on the phone. But much more revealing was how the ambient sound of a wooden chair sliding across linoleum floor made Charlie's heart ache. The fact that he was with his kids only half the time hadn't provoked him to make every second significant, which is what he'd thought would happen, but instead caused him to honour the moments that were unremarkable. Because these everyday moments now happened only half as often, Charlie had begun to find them twice as significant. Which is why the sound of the chair scraping across the kitchen floor almost reduced him to tears.

'I don't know what you want to do with the kids.' Linda didn't notice that Charlie was near tears. Or she was good enough not to mention it if she had. 'They can go over to your place early, or they can stay here. It doesn't matter to me. Why don't you text them and tell them what you want to do? But don't forget Mark has karate at seven. His uniform is in the yellow bag.'

'It's at eight. They moved the time.'

'I've got a work call coming in. Gotta go.'

'Can I just ask you one thing?'

'Quickly.'

'Do you still love me?' Charlie, still slightly burst open by the sound of the wooden chair on the floor, had been unable to stop himself from asking this. He listened to a silence that was interrupted only by the ticking.

'Listen, Charlie. I think a lot of this is about you feeling guilty. I'm your ex-wife, and I'm telling you straight out: you didn't do anything wrong. Neither of us did. We're both better people now and, more importantly, better parents. You and I lasted as long as we did. And it was great while it was great, but it ended. It's over. I have accepted that. I've healed. You gotta start asking yourself why you haven't. I really do have to get this call. Don't forget about karate.'

Static came out of the walkie-talkie. Charlie hated how casually Linda talked to him. It was a recent development. She used to be angry, and then she was perpetually disappointed, treating him as she would a younger sibling. Realizing that she no longer treated him either of these ways made Charlie feel anxious. His anxiety grew. It was a deep, thick anxiety, unlike anything he had ever felt before. It spread quickly. It coated all of his thoughts. The list of contributing factors grew: having to find Twiggy's heart in twenty-four hours, having to have the right kind of epiphany, needing to get out of Metaphoria in time to get the kids to karate. All of these things increased Charlie's anxiety. His breathing became rapid and shallow. He began sweating. A slight tremble came into his hands. Feeling dizzy, Charlie looked down at the floor and noticed that it was getting closer. He looked up and saw that the ceiling was moving farther away. It took him several moments before he realized that he had begun to shrink.

4

THE CONSEQUENCES OF DOUBT

The cuffs of Charlie Waterfield's shirt slid over his hands. His watch slid off his wrist. His pants bunched up around his ankles. Charlie tried not to panic. He failed. His panic increased how quickly he shrank. The black-and-white floor tiles rushed toward him. His jacket and then his dress shirt slipped from his rapidly diminishing shoulders. At his present rate of shrinking, Charlie would disappear in less than a minute. It was at this moment that he saw his reflection in the blade of the knife Shirley Miller had dropped on the floor.

The blade of the knife rested against the leg of the desk, so that as Charlie looked down, his reflection looked directly at him. As Charlie continued shrinking, his reflection grew larger and larger. It was impossible to determine whether this was a trick of light and reflective surfaces or whether it was actually happening. When he realized that the dried blood along the edge of the knife was his, Charlie looked away. He continued shrinking. It was desperation that compelled Charlie to look back at the knife, and when he did, his reflection began acting independently.

'Hope is a weapon, most often used against oneself,' Charlie's reflection said.

'What the hell does that mean?'

'You'll get it.'

'That is not helping.'

'Yes it is. Breathe. Just breathe. Breathe in, hold it, let it tumble out of your lungs like water in a stream.'

'Jesus! Enough! Give me something I can use!'

'I'm trying to!'

Charlie did not feel like he had enough time to experiment with his reflection's suggestion. But he didn't have any other ideas. He continued shrinking. His rate of shrinking increased even more. Becoming desperate, Charlie took a large breath. He kept it in, then he let it tumble out of his lungs like water in a stream. Doing this made him feel extremely embarrassed, but he had to admit it also made him feel better. Charlie's rate of shrinking slowed, although it did not cease.

'What I'm trying to suggest is that commonly held notions and conceptions of hope, ones you obviously entirely agree with, could very well be flawed. Are you open to that idea?'

'You're saying that hope is a bad thing?'

'I'm saying that hope is a many-sided thing. I'm saying that hope is a very powerful force. And like all powerful forces, it can be used for good or bad, constructively or destructively. Hope's function changes depending on the needs of the person holding on to it.'

'Even in Metaphoria?'

'Even more so.'

'You're telling me to give up hope?'

'I'm telling you to question your intent. I'm asking you to think about how you're using hope. I'm suggesting — and sorry, you'll have to forgive me but there is no other way to say this — that you need to becoming motivated not so much by hope, but by following your heart.'

'Easier said than done.'

'Yes, but there is a trick to following your heart.'

'Care to pass it on?'

'You have to give up all belief that you can control where it's heading.'

Charlie Waterfield felt this was true. As far as advice goes, it was more abstract than he'd have liked, but nonetheless the words of his reflection in the blade of the knife that had recently cut out his heart had a calming effect. Charlie closed his eyes. He took a deep breath. He couldn't ignore the ticking, but he was able to lower his response when each tick happened. He took a second deep breath and then a third. On the fourth, the sound of the ticking in his ears became almost soothing; the metronomic pace brought order to Charlie's speeding thoughts. His fingers got longer. His toes pushed outward. His legs increased in length.

Charlie returned to his original size. He gathered his clothes. He dressed. He sat on the chair behind the desk and tied his shoes, thinking about what his reflection had said, that he needed to rethink his ideas on hope. Charlie knew he needed to do this. He could feel it in his heart.

But exactly where his heart was, he did not know.

5

THE N.E.E.D.

The Tachycardia Tower was the tallest building in all of Metaphoria, ninety-nine storeys of steel and glass that rose upward without hesitation or compassion. The windows were always clean. The sidewalk in front of it was made of gold. The revolving door let some people in and turned others away. Occasionally people inside the building would stand at the windows and look out, their faces blank and impossible to read. The building stood at the corner of Wealth and Acquisition, the very heart of the Never-Ever-Enough District, and was considered the most prestigious address in all of Metaphoria. It attracted the city's wealthiest, most powerful people, prosperous and well-respected citizens who had lived here for years, if not decades, and who had acquired great influence, if rather miserable lives, by never questioning their motives.

Charlie didn't know any of that. He just didn't like the look of the building. Typically, he appreciated this form of architecture. He loved the unembellished lines of the glass-and-steel box. But there was something about this building that just didn't sit right with him. It wasn't only that the building felt cold, or how it conveyed aloofness as it looked down on all the other buildings surrounding it. To Charlie, the building felt untrustworthy, a feeling he'd never had about a building before. He couldn't specifically say why he felt the building was untrustworthy, but the sensation was so strong that Charlie wondered if someone who spent their days working in such a place could have a heart to lose.

Charlie parked in the shadow of the Tachycardia Tower. He'd been surprised that his position as the sole detective of the Epiphany Detective Agency had come with a car. Shortly after returning to his original height, Charlie had discovered a set of car keys hanging to the right of the office door. He was even more surprised to learn they unlocked the apple-red Corvette parked in front of the building. It was with a teenaged glee that Charlie started the engine and drove, guided by some kind of instinct, directly to the N.E.E.D. From across the street he watched the revolving door of the Tachycardia Tower, hoping to see Twiggy. He left the car running. He gunned the engine several times, just to hear the horsepower. It was while he was doing this that Charlie realized the car was the physical manifestation of a mid-life crisis.

Charlie wanted to be in any other vehicle than this one, but Metaphoria wouldn't comply. His car remained an apple-red 1984 Corvette. Slumping down in the driver's sea,t Charlie watched people exit the building and tried not to listen too closely to the ticking, while trying to figure out how to proceed. Shirley had given Charlie only her husband's nickname and not a physical description, so he didn't know exactly who he was looking for until a man came through the revolving door whose arms were made of twigs. Eight sticks, twisted together, formed his arms. The sticks bent halfway down, making elbows. Ten tiny twigs served as fingers.

Twiggy raised his left stick and hailed a taxi. As soon as he got inside, the cab started giving off a pulsating red glow. This made it easy for Charlie to follow the car, although he quickly became disoriented by the way the city streets were laid out. Many of the intersections weren't formed by two streets crossing but by a fork, where the road veered off in two directions. This made it difficult for Charlie to keep track of what direction he had headed in. The length of each block varied wildly, making it impossible to know how far they'd actually travelled. Charlie was already lost when the taxi hung a left onto a street that was a downward spiral.

The spiral street continued for some time. Just when Charlie lost hope that it would ever end, it did. They drove into a dark tunnel. Charlie turned on his lights. The tunnel also seemed to go on forever and, at the very moment that Charlie started to believe *it* would never end, he drove out of the tunnel and into bright afternoon sunlight. Blinking and confused, he continued following the taxi. They drove past a sign that announced what part of Metaphoria they were in.

The sign said

FORGOTTEN TOWN

Forget yourself in Forgotten Town!

Forgotten Town was not just abandoned but deconstructed. The foundations of buildings that were no longer standing were all that remained. There were no trees or parked cars or signs of human activity. Charlie hung back so the taxi he was following wouldn't see him. He watched the cab stop in front of the only structure within view, a one-storey building made of cinder blocks. The windows were narrow and barred. The building was surrounded by a chain-link fence topped with barbed wire. A tall black iron gate in front of the entrance hung open.

The sign in front of it said

THE PRISON OF OPTIONAL INCARCERATION
NECESSARY TO TERMINATE OR LOWER
EXCESSIVE SHAME AND SELF-REPROACH

Charlie watched Twiggy go inside. The taxi pulled away. The building radiated the colour grey – everything within a thirty-metre radius, even the grass, even Twiggy as he approached the entrance, was drained of colour. Twiggy went inside. Charlie pulled into the parking lot. He gripped the steering wheel tightly. The sound of the ticking got louder. Charlie turned on the radio. He increased the volume, engaged the windshield wipers, and set the heater to the maximum setting. All of these things failed to drown out the sound of the ticking. Charlie waited ten more minutes, just to be sure he wouldn't run into Twiggy, then he got out of the car and walked across the deserted parking lot. As he got closer to the Prison of Optional Incarceration Necessary to Terminate or Lower Excessive Shame and Self-Reproach, the colours of his clothes got duller. When he reached the entrance, his shoes were no longer brown and his tie was no longer green. Everything everywhere was varying shades of grey. Charlie tried the front door and, finding it unlocked, went inside.

The ceilings were so low that Charlie, who was not tall, had to lean forward to avoid striking them with the crown of his head. The walls were drywall but painted to look like cinder blocks. The absence of colour continued.

The building consisted of one long hallway, which Charlie couldn't see the end of. He walked down this hallway and came to several barred doors, all unlocked. Along both sides of this hallway, ten metres apart, were identical cells. Each cell held a prisoner. Each prisoner held the same position: they sat on the edge of their cots with their feet flat on the ground, their shoulders rounded and hunched, and their forearms flat against their upper thighs. They all stared at the floor. Not one of them looked up as Charlie walked past.

Twiggy came out of a cell about three hundred metres in front of Charlie. Charlie ducked into an empty cell and stared at the floor. He didn't look up as Twiggy walked past. When Charlie could no longer hear Twiggy's footsteps, he left that cell and walked to the one Twiggy had just left. The door slid open easily. The prisoner's hair had been recently cut and his double-breasted jacket was well tailored, although both his haircut and suit were several years out of fashion.

Charlie recognized the prisoner immediately. His name was Wolff Parkinson White, and he'd been in a committed relationship with Linda Penmore until she'd fallen in love with Charlie and married him. The last time he'd seen him, Wolff had tried to pick a fight. Charlie waited for him to look up. Wolff continued staring at the stains on the concrete floor. When Wolff did look up, he initially failed to recognize Charlie, as if his eyes were so accustomed to staring at the same piece of floor that they'd lost the ability to perceive anything new.

'Charlie Waterfield! Not surprised to see you here.' Wolff shuffled to his left, making room for Charlie on the cot.

Charlie sat down and took his cigarettes from the inside pocket of his jacket. His fingers trembled as he fought with the packaging. The first cigarette he pulled out fell onto the floor. The second he passed to Wolff. The third he successfully lit. He passed his lighter to Wolff. Neither talked. The ash from Wolff's cigarette turned to snow just before it hit the floor.

'How long have you been in Metaphoria?' Wolff asked.

'About an hour.'

'Wow. Well, don't worry about panicking. Everybody panics when they first get here.'

'I've already almost died because of shrinking. And I have a bomb in my chest where my heart should be.'

'Welcome to Metaphoria!'

'How long have *you* been here?'

'I'm afraid I can't answer that.'

'I won't judge.'

'I wish I could tell you. I can't even remember how long I've been sitting in this cell. Tell me – what did you arrive as?'

'I'm not following you, Wolff.'

'Everyone, when they arrive in Metaphoria, gets some sort of strange profession. Something they didn't – something no one did, back home. Something more out of fiction than real life. What's yours?'

'A detective. I work for the Epiphany Detective Agency. I think it's mine. As in, I *am* the Epiphany Detective Agency.'

'Then I suppose you have some questions.'

'I do.'

'Ask away, although I don't think there's much you don't already know about me.'

'I'm more interested in the guy who just visited you.'

'Twiggy?'

'Yeah. Him. Who is he to you?'

'He's my brother.'

'I didn't know you had a brother.'

'I didn't until I got here.'

'Is he a good guy?'

'No. Absolutely not.'

'Do you know his wife?'

'Which one?'

'He has other wives?'

'Two.'

'Shirley Miller's his third?'

'Technically she's his first, third, and fifth. They've been married three times and divorced twice. They've got one of those loves that runs hot and cold.'

'Do you think he still loves her?'

'That's the thing about love, isn't it? Even in Metaphoria there's no indicator light that flashes green, no absolute way of knowing if someone's got love in their heart for you or not.'

'Wouldn't that be nice.'

'A dream.'

'Is your brother a careful man? Would he be prone to lose something?'

'The only thing he's ever lost are his arms. And they grew back.'

'Do you know anybody who'd want to steal your brother's heart?'

'I know he has a tendency to give it away.'

'Anybody in particular?'

'The name Kitty Packesel comes to mind. She's a scientist. They're working on some kind of secret project together.

Twiggy wouldn't tell me much about it except to say it's called the Spero Machine.'

'What's it supposed to do?'

'I don't really know. Something to do with love.'

'What doesn't have to do with love in this town?'

'Why do you think I stay in this cell?'

'Anything else you can tell me about their relationship?'

'They meet every Thursday at the Disappointment.'

'The Disappointment?'

'It's a restaurant in the Seven Months Later District. Twiggy comes and visits me every Thursday, then meets her for dinner. They'll just be sitting down for appetizers right now.'

'I appreciate your candour, Wolff.'

'Well, it's Metaphoria, Charlie. If you're here, there's gotta be some reason for it.'

'Let's hope so.' The cell door swung open. Charlie stood. Then he paused. 'What is this place anyway?'

'Don't think of it as a place but as an opportunity.'

'To do what?'

'Has anyone explained to you how to get out of Metaphoria?'

'I was told I had to have an epiphany. That it was best to form it as a question, to try and find the purpose of the human heart.'

'What if all that's wrong? What if the secret to triggering a poof isn't an epiphany at all? What if it isn't about self-realization but punishment? Technically this is a prison, but there are no trials, judges, or convictions. There aren't even locks or guards. Incarceration is entirely voluntarily. This whole building is an opportunity to do your time for whatever it is that you've done wrong.'

'So you just sit here and wait for your poof to happen?'

'Exactly.'

'Now I understand the acronym.'

Charlie nodded as he left Wolff's cell. Wolff looked back at the stains on the concrete floor. He didn't look up as Charlie walked away.

Charlie had almost retraced his steps completely when he noticed the cell. He still thought this place was ludicrous, but something strange and powerful pulled him toward the empty cell. He stopped in front of the door. Unable to resist, Charlie gave it a gentle push. The door drifted open and he stepped inside.

The cot creaked as Charlie sat down. He rested his forearms on the tops of his legs. He looked down at the floor. He thought about Wanda and how he hadn't used the walkie-talkie to call her. He thought about how unlikely it was that he was going to get his kids to karate. These things weighed heavily on his mind, then the cell door swung closed, causing a sudden metallic clang to ring out. It was at this moment that Charlie felt the heavy weight of his obligations, expectations, and responsibilities leave his body. He breathed deeply in. He noticed how shallow his breaths had been. He was unsure how long he had been breathing this way, perhaps years.

Since the P.O.I.N.T.L.E.S.S. had no guards or locks, the length of his sentence was entirely up to Charlie. The more years he imagined giving himself, the better he felt. It was as Charlie contemplated giving himself a life sentence, when he saw himself spending the rest of his life in this tiny, windowless cell, that every ounce of his remorse, guilt, and shame faded away and he decided that he would never, ever leave this cell.

6

THE UNNAMED GHOST

It was the air conditioner that saved Charlie Waterfield. The overwhelming silence created when the machine cycled off made the ticking in his ears insufferably loud. The ticking was so loud it became impossible for Charlie to think about anything else but the ticking, how each tick brought him a second closer to the moment when the bomb would explode, and that this moment, should he fail to find Twiggy's heart, would come in less than twenty-four hours.

Charlie wasn't sure how long his sentence should be, but he knew twenty-four hours wasn't nearly enough. He stood up and gave the door of his cell a gentle push. It swung open, easily. Charlie stepped into the hallway. He closed the cell door behind him. The moment it clanked shut, Charlie's remorse, guilt, and shame returned. This being Metaphoria, the weight of these things made Charlie's knees buckle. He staggered in the hallway.

All the prisoners looked up as Charlie stumbled down the corridor. Embarrassed, he pretended he didn't see them. He looked at his watch.

The watch said:

23 HR 19 MIN 57 SEC

By the time Charlie got to his car, he stank of grief. The engine wouldn't start. He turned the key again and again, but the motor did nothing but cough. He hit the steering wheel with the open palm of his hand. This felt good, so Charlie did it again. He did it several more times. Having spent his anger, Charlie closed his eyes. He took a deep breath, held it in his lungs, then let it out like water in a river. He continued doing this until a sad calm took the spot where the anger used to be. Then he turned the key and the car started on the first try.

As he drove away, Charlie looked at the P.O.I.N.T.L.E.S.S. in his rear-view mirror. The look was filled with longing. He drove at a leisurely pace, ignoring the honks of the drivers behind him, choosing streets randomly, based on whether or not he liked the buildings on them. Charlie didn't try to find his way to the Disappointment. He considered that an impossible task. He made a firm decision to spend the next twenty-three hours and nineteen minutes driving the streets of Metaphoria. Something inside his heart said this would be a good way to go, even though he didn't exactly know where his heart was. It was at this point that a ghost materialized in the passenger seat.

Exactly what this was the ghost of, Charlie couldn't tell. The Ghost was certainly handsome. His jaw was square. His features were symmetrical. His hair was black and thick and floated above his head as if he were underwater. The only unappealing thing about the Ghost was the chains that encircled his waist and chest and bound his hands behind his back, which must have made sitting in the passenger seat extremely uncomfortable. The chains were thick and heavy, although they gave off an orange glow and a sickly sweet smell of rotting oranges.

'Do you know who I am?' The Ghost's voice was deep and resonant and as pretty as his face. Charlie noticed how the Ghost's transparency increased and decreased with his breathing, and that even though his hands were tied uncomfortably behind his back, his expression held a calm openness. But Charlie was unable to identify what he was the ghost of. Knowing from experience how vitally important it is to know which ghost is haunting you, Charlie become anxious.

'Can you tell me?'

'That's not the way it works here.'

'What's the point of that?'

'In this instance it will be more powerful if you figure it out for yourself.'

'Why?'

'You'll just have to trust me.'

'You don't know, do you?'

'You will just have to trust me.'

'Do you not know what ghost you are?'

'Of course I do!' The Ghost became angry. This somehow made him more handsome. 'How is your wife faring with the divorce?'

'I don't want to talk about that.'

The Ghost rattled his chains. Although he was strikingly handsome and completely incapacitated by the heavy chains that encircled his body, the gesture terrified Charlie.

'It's been hard on both of us.'

'Tell the truth!'

'It's a difficult time.'

'The truth!'

'She's doing ... good.'

'All things considered, she's doing quite well, isn't she?'

'Maybe.'

'You're the one who's having a hard time moving on. Is that right?'

'I guess.'

'You're still hoping to get back together with her, aren't you?'

'No.'

'Do not lie to me!'

'I'm not!'

'Can it be? Do you not even realize it?'

'Realize what? What am I not realizing?'

'Do you even want to get back home?'

'Of course I do!'

'Then stop hiding in your hope!'

'I don't even feel like I have any hope at all!'

'Do you really not see it? That wanting, hoping, to rekindle your marriage is nothing but burrowing your head in emotional topsoil? Creating a fallout shelter and stocking it with enough loneliness and hurt and shame to outlast the emotional Armageddon? You are coddling your sorrow and grief, Charlie Waterfield! Why? Because it's safer! As long as you're hoping to get back together with your wife, as long as you're recovering from your divorce, you will never have to make yourself emotionally vulnerable. You will never have to love again.

'Is it safer? Of course it is. But the consequences, besides the fact that you are living without love, wasting your hope on something that will never happen and would be unsustainable if it ever were to chance into existence, is that you have turned your life into a waiting room.

'Is that really want you want?'

'Are you the ghost of the love I have for my wife?'

'Oh, Charlie. Still using the present tense? Are you really that bad off?' The look of great frustration on the Unnamed Ghost's face melted to compassion. 'Let me give you a hint. Stop right now!'

Slightly enchanted by the Unnamed Ghost, Charlie did as it demanded. He slammed on the brakes. The car jerked to a sudden stop. Looking to his left, Charlie discovered he had stopped in front of the Disappointment. When he looked back to his right, the Unnamed Ghost was gone.

7

A RAISED CURSIVE FONT

The Disappointment was just west of Unrealistic and Expectation, quite close to the offices of the Epiphany Detective Agency. Charlie put the Corvette keys in his pocket and went inside. The restaurant was large and the interior design was so minimalist that Charlie worried a slight tilt in the earth would send him sliding down the polished marble floors and granite tabletops, with nothing to hold on to. There were more than fifty tables. They were all set for two. Every table was occupied by a couple.

None of the couples held hands. Few looked each other in the eye. Nobody was enjoying themselves. All the couples sat across from each other, arguing in their own unique way. Some yelled at each other. At other tables, one partner struggled to hold back tears while the other attempted to convey something complicated and hurtful. But by far the saddest couples, as far as Charlie was concerned, were the ones who weren't saying anything to each other, the candles flickering in front of them as they silently stared at entrees that had already turned cold.

Charlie took a seat at the bar. It did not take long to spot Twiggy. Sitting at a table near the window, Twiggy's sticks flew wildly about as he attempted to articulate something, but Charlie couldn't figure out what. He assumed that the woman sitting across from Twiggy was Kitty, since she had a tail. Kitty's neutral expression held the impenetrable confidence of a locked safe, but her tail beat the floor with a building intensity that cresendoed as she tossed her drink in Twiggy's face.

Several drops of apple-red margarita slid down Twiggy's cheek, and he pushed these into his mouth with the longest twig on his right hand. His smile was disturbing. It failed to convey compassion or empathy or even a small amount of affection. Twiggy threw money on the table. The bills landed on the white linen tablecloth like geese on a pond. Kitty and Twiggy stood up. Twiggy left the restaurant and Kitty came to the bar. She took the seat beside Charlie.

'Is he watching me?' Kitty nodded toward the long mirror that hung above the bar. Twiggy was reflected in it. He stood on the sidewalk, looking in. A small purple flame rose from Twiggy's chest.

'He seems to be watching us.'

'Is his chest on fire?'

'Yes.'

'What colour are the flames?'

'There's only one flame.'

'Are you sure?'

'I am.'

'What colour is it?'

'Mauve?'

'Good.'

'Why is it good?'

'His dignity burns purple. It'll be gone soon.'

Charlie looked back into the mirror. Twiggy remained perfectly still as the purple flame got smaller and smaller.

When it disappeared, Twiggy put his twigs in his pockets and walked away.

'He seems pretty sad for a man without a heart,' Charlie said.

'He's as sad about losing me as he would be about his second-favourite watch.'

'I don't think we've been introduced.'

'I know who you are and who you're working for, Mr. Waterfield. I know that she's charged you to find Twiggy's heart. I also know what she's done to you.' Kitty opened her hand and pressed it flat against Charlie's chest. She kept it there for three ticks longer than she needed to.

'You seem to know a lot about Shirley Miller's business.'

'We have a common interest.'

'Which is?'

'Her husband's heart.'

'A friend of mine thought you might already have it.'

'Unfortunately, no. Twiggy's name has not been written upon me. Check if you want to.'

Kitty turned her back to Charlie. She lifted the bottom of her shirt and swished her tail out of the way. Written on her skin, straddling her backbone, was a list of seventeen names, all in the same raised cursive font. Kitty undid her bra strap, ensuring that no names would be concealed.

'What are these?'

'You don't know? How long have you been here?'

'In Metaphoria?' Charlie looked at his watch. 'Two hours fifteen minutes.'

'You're having quite a day.'

'I'm trying not to panic.'

'It's okay. Everybody panics here.'

'Even you?'

'Especially me.'

'And the names?'

'In Metaphoria, the name of every person you become intimate with appears in a raised cursive font on your back. The last name on the list is the most recent and always sits in the very same place, just above the small of your back. When a new name appears, the rest of the list shifts upward like text written on a typewriter, the font size changing to accommodate the length.'

'That must lead to some awkward moments.'

'That's not the hard part.'

'How can it get worse?'

'It is almost impossible to predict what constitutes intimacy around here. It's not so simple as allowing someone to insert some part of themselves into some part of you. Nor does it seem based on the depth of emotional attachment. Sometimes it takes years for someone's name to appear on your back. Sometimes a name appears from as brief an encounter as a shared elevator ride. Although it never seems random. When a name appears, it never comes as a surprise.'

Charlie read Kitty's back. The names were numerous. None of them were Twiggy's.

'Your turn.' Kitty lowered her shirt. She lit a cigarette and puffed a series of heart-shaped smoke rings into the air.

'Do the names hold over from back home?'

'No. It only happens with citizens of Metaphoria.'

'Well, then there'll be no one there.'

'Let's just check?'

Kitty spun Charlie's stool around and untucked his shirt. She used her tail to lift it and the back of his jacket. She ran the tips of her fingers across the skin at the small of his back.

'You may have only been here for two hours but you've been busy, Charlie. Wanda Parks? And who is Linda Penmore?'

'Jesus. My ex-wife.'

'And you arrived together?'

'She doesn't live here.'

'I've never heard of that,' Kitty said. Her tail lowered Charlie's shirt and jacket. She spun him back around and then her tail began swishing, back and forth. She was clearly upset. 'I've never heard of the name of someone not living in Metaphoria appearing on the skin of someone who was. Do you love this Linda?'

'That's a complicated question.'

'When isn't it?'

'Do you love Twiggy?'

'I do.'

'That doesn't sound very complicated.'

'He doesn't love me. That's the complicated part.'

'Do you think he still loves his wife?'

'I suspect he does. But how would anyone ever know something like that for sure? Even here in Metaphoria, it's not like there's some sort of indicator light that flashes green on the small of our arm, telling us our love is true.'

'Wouldn't that be nice.'

'You still haven't answered the question.'

'I do. I love her as much as I ever have. I love her more than I ever have! I think that's why I am here.'

'That's a lot of protesting.'

'What are you implying?'

'It's never that simple, Charlie. No one in Metaphoria gets off that easy. I suspect her name is there for the opposite reason.'

'The opposite of what?'

'Not because you love her, but because you don't.'

'You're wrong about that.'

'We'll see. If you're so sure of yourself, tell me — what's the purpose of the human heart?'

'That is currently unclear to me.'

'I have a theory. I'm still here, so it can't be the right one, but I feel like I'm getting closer.'

'I'm listening.'

'The purpose of the human heart is to make us so lonely we reach out to each other.'

Kitty reached out and took Charlie's hand. Charlie held hers tightly. They leaned toward each other, pressing their cheeks together. It was at this moment that the stools Charlie and Kitty sat on glided with perfect ease several feet back from the bar. Charlie and Kitty kept their cheeks against each other as the stools slipped along the polished marble floor across the restaurant. They glided out the door and across the sidewalk and came to a slow, gentle stop directly in front of the opening door of the taxicab waiting at the curb.

8

THE SECRET WARMTH OF
KITTY PACKESEL'S APARTMENT

In Metaphoria, taxi drivers consider the journey the desti-
nation. Maybe taxi drivers everywhere think this, but in
Metaphoria they take it seriously. Every ride is a spiritual
journey. In Metaphoria, taxi drivers do not ask ask where
their fares want to go. They never start the meter and they
never look in the rear-view mirror. They simply pull away
from the curb and begin to drive like their fate depends on
it. Charlie, who didn't know any of this, was alarmed by
how recklessly the cabbie was driving. His anxiety began to
rise. He could feel himself start to shrink. Then the right
side of the back seat tilted upward at a seventy-degree angle,
causing Kitty to slide toward him. While this didn't lower
Charlie's anxiety, it certainly captured his attention. Kitty
looked at Charlie. She ran her fingers through his hair. She
tilted her head slightly to the left. When their lips touched,
the back seat reclined. The roof, doors, and windows disappeared as the taxi turned into a heart-shaped bed.

The deeper Charlie and Kitty kissed, the faster the bed
travelled. Oncoming headlights became blurs of colour.
Street lights were a single white streak. It started to snow.
Snowflakes got caught in Charlie's hair and the folds of
Kitty's dress. The snow began falling harder. They kissed
deeper. The storm turned into a blizzard. Their hands were
given free rein. Charlie climbed on top of Kitty.

'Stop!' Kitty said.

The cab had been travelling so quickly, and it stopped so suddenly, that Charlie became disoriented. He shook his head. Snow still clung to his eyelids and hair. Kitty rolled through the snow and off the heart-shaped bed. Charlie did the same. As the taxi raced away, it turned back into a regular car. Charlie looked around – strings of multi-coloured lights with burnt-out bulbs hung in every window. Mittenless children wearing T-shirts and jeans stood on the corner, singing 'Silent Night.' They sang as poorly as they were dressed for the weather. A man in a Santa suit bumped into Charlie, failed to look up, and drank from a mickey of rum as he staggered onward.

'Where are we?'

Kitty pointed to a sign across the street.

THE SAD CHRISTMAS DISTRICT:
The Christmas you can never forget …

Thus prompted, Charlie noticed other things. Every living room he could see into held a Christmas tree, but all the trees were short and missing limbs, the sort of trees that would have been the last to sell. He counted four different men wearing threadbare suits and sitting on their front steps with their heads in their hands. Two of these men were sobbing. At the end of Kitty's block, someone broke the passenger window of a parked car, gathered up the presents, and ran away.

'Why do you live here?'

'It reminds me of my childhood.'

Kitty stepped closer to Charlie, wrapped her arms around his shoulders, and held him tightly. Charlie did the same to her. Several times Charlie thought Kitty was about to end their embrace. Each time she didn't, he felt a significant portion of his loneliness leave his body and go into hers. At the same time, an equal amount of Kitty's loneliness left her body and went into his. Charlie no longer felt the need to sleep with Kitty. He understood, with great clarity, that this was what all his casual sexual encounters had always been about. As the embrace continued, the door of Kitty's building opened, and a strong winter wind lifted them and carried them up the stairs toward her apartment.

The door of Kitty's apartment flew open. She and Charlie continued holding each other. They were just past the threshold, although still a metre above the floor, when the wind ceased to blow. It was not a graceful landing. They crashed onto the thick white carpet. The impact was severe. Both were knocked unconscious. They remained unconscious for some time.

Kitty was the first to recover. She got up and dimmed the lights, lit a fire and candles. She lay down beside Charlie and held him tightly. When he started waking up, she let him go. They smiled at each other as the radiators began clanging.

'You have to go.' Kitty stood. She straightened her clothes, took Charlie's hand, and pulled him to his feet. Putting both of her palms back on his chest, she pushed Charlie toward the door.

'Why? What?' Charlie noticed that the room had suddenly become unbearably hot. Much more so than could be explained by the raging fire.

'Now. Go.'

'Is it the kissing? Because that doesn't count. I wasn't really kissing you. It wasn't real kissing. I just wanted you to start trusting me because I want to ask you questions about Twiggy.'

'Let's just say it is.'

'To be completely honest with you, I'm not just here because I'm sexually attracted to you. I mean, the truth, the complete truth, is that I'm recently divorced – well, not that recently – but still I'm pretty emotionally unavailable. Plus, I have this thing going on with a woman named Wanda who I really like. In fact, I actually love. And I think that kinda frightens me, that I love her. But what I'd really like to do is ask you more questions about Twiggy Miller. Can I do that? I mean, I think I'm in a terrible situation. Why am I being so honest?'

'They heat my apartment with truth. If I'd realized it was so cold out, I would have insisted you leave.'

'Are you trying to hide something?'

'Who isn't?'

'Is it about Twiggy's heart?'

'They wouldn't like it if I told you that.'

'Who's they?'

'They wouldn't like it if I told you that either.'

'Do you know where his heart is?'

'If you go after his heart, you will be putting yourself in terrible danger.'

'If I don't, the bomb in my chest explodes.'

'I won't betray his trust.'

'Your loyalties are misplaced. You can do better than Twiggy.'

'You really believe that?'

'I don't think either of us is capable of lying right now. Will you tell me where Twiggy's heart is?'

'The reason Shirley can't find his heart is because he's stored it outside of his body. At a place called Forever Yours, the most prestigious cardiac self-storage facility in Metaphoria, located at Pride and Power, deep in the Never-Ever-Enough District. Unit #117.'

'How can I thank you?'

'Tell me why you're so sad.'

'It was supposed to last forever.'

'What was?'

'My marriage.'

'You're caught in a myth, Charlie.'

'Only one?'

'Love isn't this indestructible force. Love, like any human creation, ends. Those who can't accept that are destined to live a lie.'

'Even if that's true, why didn't mine last longer?'

'Because that's not the kind of love it was.'

'But I wanted it to last forever.'

'Why?'

Charlie had to think about that one. Several answers came immediately to mind, but he could not voice them because they weren't true.

'Because it hurts so much when it ends,' he finally said.

'Oh, Charlie. A love that lasts forever generates just as much, if not more, heartache, sorrow, and sadness as one that doesn't.' As Kitty spoke these words, she realized they were true.

'Anything else you feel like sharing?' Charlie asked.

'I'm working with the W.B.C.'

'The what?'

'The White Blood Cells? You haven't heard of us?'

'I'm new in town.'

'You need to be careful, Charlie. We know who you are. And we're watching you.'

'Jesus. What do you want?'

'We want what everyone here wants.'

'Which is?'

'The full expression of the human heart! Because only the full expression of the human heart will lead to finding the purpose of the human heart!'

'What is the purpose of the human heart?'

'I used to think the purpose of the human heart was to make us so lonely that we reach out to each other. But, just now, I've changed my mind. I don't think that's right anymore. The purpose of the human heart is to make us strong enough that we can reach out to each other!'

Kitty looked right at Charlie, but her eyes were focused on something invisible and very far away.

Poof!

8

THE CYCLOPS

Charlie stood in the middle of Kitty's living room, trying to come to terms with what he'd just seen. The purple smoke cleared. The smell of burning cedar lingered in the air and then it too disappeared. Although it took more than a few moments, Charlie realized he'd just witnessed a poof. This was the first time his circumstances hadn't felt doomed since Shirley had cut out his heart. It was at this precise moment that the door to Kitty's apartment opened and the white shag carpet started to move in swells, like deep water on the open sea. The waves swept Charlie out of the living room and into the hallway. The door closed, all on its own.

Charlie walked down the stairs and onto the street. It was no longer snowing. The soft, fluffy white snow on the ground was already melting, turning into a dirty, thick slush. Charlie's joy at so easily finding the location of Twiggy's heart was tempered by the fact that he remained in the Sad Christmas District, a very sorrowful place. Another drunken Santa bumped into Charlie's shoulder. A faint mewing came from inside the bag over his shoulder. This made Charlie shudder. The street lights flickered in time to 'Jingle Bells.' The sad eyes of an elderly woman watched Charlie through dirty faded curtains as they waited for relatives who would never arrive. Drunken men stopped on street corners, struggling to maintain their balance as they stared at the wrinkled photographs of their children clutched in their hands.

Charlie walked slowly. He thought about his own children. He contemplated the Christmases he'd provided for them and concluded that they were only marginally better than this one. He did not try to hail the many cabs that splashed slush onto his pant legs as they raced by. He didn't think he deserved the luxury of a cab ride. He just kept walking. With every step, his spirits sank a little bit more and the ticking in his ears got a tiny bit louder. He was practically deaf and barely holding back his tears as he neared the parking lot of the Disappointment. Unable to resist any longer, Charlie raised his arm. He looked at his wrist:

19 HR 14 MIN 15 SEC

Knowing how quickly time was passing did not make Charlie walk any faster. His car was the only one left in Disappointment parking lot. He got the keys out of his pocket and noticed a Cyclops lumbering toward him. The Cyclops appeared to be angry, although it was hard to decipher the look in his eye.

'You Charlie Waterfield?' the Cyclops asked.

'No?'

'Is this your car?'

'A red Corvette? I would think not.'

'Then why are there car keys in your hand?"

'Okay. So it is my car. But I'm not Charlie Waterfield.'

'Oh, I think you are, Charlie.' The Cyclops put two fingers under Charlie's chin and with very little effort lifted him off the ground.

'Want to know how I know you're Waterfield?'

Charlie didn't respond. His feet kicked at everything that wasn't there.

'Because you're an idiot. Only an idiot would sleep with a Cyclops's wife.'

'Wanda's married?'

A look of shock and hurt crossed the Cyclops's face. It stayed there for several moments. Charlie stopped kicking at nothing. He recognized that look. He knew how much hurt it took to provoke it. Charlie's empathy went out to the poor wounded giant. The Cyclops took his fingers away and Charlie crashed to the sidewalk. He didn't look up as the Cyclops started to cry. The creature's tears landed on Charlie's head, drenching him.

Not knowing what else to do, Charlie reached up and took the Cyclops's hand. It was an odd thing to do, but the Cyclops seemed to appreciate the gesture. He held Charlie's hand tightly. Charlie saw a lot of himself in the Cyclops. It was easy to imagine what the Cyclops was feeling; Charlie had been there before. In fact, this was the first time he had been the other in a relationship. On all other occasions, Charlie had been in the Cyclops's position. He had to admit that it felt better being the one on this side, although not by as big a degree as he'd imagined.

Charlie tugged on the Cyclops's hand until he sat down beside him. They leaned against the front bumper of Charlie's car. Charlie took out his pack of Ten Pints. He gave one to the Cyclops.

'I have to have two or I get nothing from it,' said the Cyclops.

Charlie shook out another cigarette. He lit all three and passed two to the Cyclops. They smoked in silence. Charlie noticed that the ash in the Cyclops's cigarettes turned to snow just before it hit the ground.

'Here's an idea,' Charlie said. 'Maybe it's a myth that love is supposed to last forever. Maybe love isn't indestructible. Some loves last longer than others, but all of them end.'

'I wanted mine to last forever.'

'I wanted that too. But how do we know a love that lasts forever doesn't cause more pain than one that ends? Or is even as tender and rewarding? There's a lot more evidence that the opposite is true.'

'Doesn't a love that ends mean it wasn't a true love in the first place?'

'I hadn't really thought about that.' Charlie became lost in thought. He closed his eyes. When he opened them again, the Cyclops's fist was centimetres from his face. Charlie threw up his hands and shut his eyes. Several moments passed. No punch landed. Charlie looked up. Directly in front of him was the Cyclops's open palm. In the middle of it was a wedding ring.

'Next time you see Wanda, you give her this.'

The Cyclops dropped his wedding ring. It fell to the sidewalk and left a heart-shaped impression in the concrete. Then the Cyclops walked away. Charlie traced the heart-shaped divot with his index finger.

He stared at the ring for twenty-six minutes, which, considering how few minutes Charlie had left, was a very long time.

9

THE OTHER CHANNEL

The Cyclops's ring was pure gold, heavy, and very slippery. Charlie's fingers failed to find purchase on his first three attempts to lift it. There was a small gap between the bottom of the ring and the heart-shaped dent it had put in the sidewalk. Sliding his fingers in there, Charlie was able to get a good enough grip to lift the ring onto its side. It took all of his strength to do this.

Out of breath, Charlie rolled the ring along the sidewalk to his car. He opened the trunk, grabbed the sides of the ring, and lifted with his knees. He gave it everything he had, but it wasn't enough to lift the ring into the trunk. Charlie rolled the ring back to the sidewalk.

'Sorry.'

Charlie got into his car. He started the engine. He put the car into gear, but when he pushed down on the gas pedal nothing happened. Taking the car back out of gear, Charlie shut down the engine. He walked back to the ring and searched the trunk, hoping to find something he could use. This impulse was rewarded. In the back of the trunk was a long length of chain. The links were thick and heavy. They gave off an orange glow and the sickly sweet smell of rotting oranges. Charlie recognized them as the same chains the Ghost had worn, so at least he knew they were strong.

Charlie slid the chain through the middle of the Cyclops's wedding ring. He looped the ends over the trailer hitch and inspected it. He tugged the chains. Everything seemed secure. He went back to his car, started the engine, put it into gear, and had just lifted his foot off the brake when the walkie-talkie let out a high-pitched bleep. Charlie dug the device out of his pocket, where it had sat since he'd left the office of the Epiphany Detective Agency.

The channel had been changed from Linda to Wanda. He wondered if it'd been switched by accident or fate. He wondered whether living in Metaphoria rendered such a question obsolete. He paused, savouring the realization that simply being alive rendered that question obsolete. This was the first epiphany Charlie had in Metaphoria. He waited to be enveloped in purple smoke and the smell of burning cedar. Neither arrived. Charlie picked up the walkie-talkie and held it close to his mouth.

'Hello? Wanda?' Charlie said eagerly.

'Charlie! How are you?'

'I've been better.' Charlie didn't know what to say next. In the resulting silence, the sound of the ticking in his ears became loud. The longer the silence continued, the louder the ticking became. And yet Charlie was unable to break the silence.

'Charlie, I'm ... I'm afraid that I might have to break our date tonight. I'm in a bit of strange place.'

'So am I.'

'I doubt yours is as strange as mine.'

'I'm pretty sure it's more.'

Although Charlie rarely bickered with Wanda, this sort of one-upmanship was standard for them. Charlie was going to let it go, until something large and colossal screamed on the other side of town. It wasn't the sound so much that disturbed Charlie – although as evidence that darker terrors existed in Metaphoria, it did send a chill through his body. What alarmed him was that the same sound came through the walkie-talkie.

'Charlie, are you … Where are you?' Wanda had heard it too.

'Are you on a walkie-talkie?'

'Are you in Metaphoria?'

'How many settings does it have?'

'Two. One for you and one for my – '

'You really are married?'

'Oh, Charlie.'

'Why a Cyclops?'

'He wasn't a Cyclops back home.'

'We're both in Metaphoria?'

'I am. How did you get here?'

'A man in a purple hat … '

' … purple smoke … '

'The smell of burning cedar.'

'Jesus.'

'Jesus.'

'Did you arrive as something?'

'I'm a detective. I have my own agency. The Epiphany Detective Agency. You?'

'Some kind of code-breaker? Adventurer, I think? Some sort of spy maybe? It's not clear. Nobody will give me any straight answer. I work at the Library of Blank Pages. I'm afraid that my life is in jeopardy.'

'I'll come as soon as I can.'

'I haven't been out of the library. I don't know what part of the city I'm in.'

'I'll find you.'

'How?'

'It's Metaphoria.'

'Right.'

'We need to talk about your husband.'

'I didn't mean to hurt you.'

'Why didn't you tell me?'

'Would you have stayed with me if I had?'

For several moments the ticking in Charlie's ears was louder than it had ever been.

'Exactly,' Wanda said.

'Can you look on the small of your back?'

'I can't ... Wait ... There's something there. I can feel it. Let me get to the bathroom...'

Through the ticking and his impatience, Charlie listened to Wanda's footsteps. He heard a door swing open and closed.

'I'm here. I'm at the mirror.' Wanda's voice had become echoey. Charlie heard the rustle of her clothes.

'What do you see there?'

'It's a name. Floral script. Hard to read backward.'

'Who does it say?'

'It's your name, Charlie. What does that mean? Wait ... I have to go.'

Before Charlie could answer, the walkie-talkie began broadcasting nothing but static. Wanda was gone. Charlie stared at the machine. He felt uneasy and anxious. The underlying sense of despondency that had been within him since Shirley had taken his heart pushed itself to the front of his consciousness. He was unable to explain the

sudden victory of all these negative emotions, until he realized this was the first time in their relationship he hadn't
hung up first.

10

THE PURPLE VELVET BAG

With the Cyclops's wedding ring dragging behind his car, the fastest Charlie could go was twenty kilometres an hour. The ring made a deafening clang and shot sparks up into the air as it repeatedly crashed against the pavement, although it still wasn't as loud as the ticking in Charlie's ears.

The ticking changed timbre depending on what part of town Charlie was driving through. On the streets of First Love Village, the ticking ticked a little faster and quieter, which made the sound warm and optimistic but slightly doomed. In Revengetown, the ticking was pounding and steady, without hesitating or missing a beat. The exact opposite happened in the Middle-Aged District, where each tick seemed to come a fraction of a second too late, sounding tentative and unsure of itself. When the ticking took on a boisterous, overconfident sound, Charlie knew he was back in the N.E.E.D. Three minutes later, Charlie found the northwest corner of Pride and Power and parked across the street.

The building that housed Forever Yours was an old bank building. It was highly fortified. Bars covered the windows. Barbed wire encircled the roof. It was so brightly lit with large, circular lamps that Charlie had to squint to look at it directly. A helicopter flew overhead.

It did not look like the kind of place he could easily break into.

Charlie remained acutely aware that every second counted – the ticking in his ears wouldn't let him forget it – but the building's impenetrability gave him permission to wait until morning. Even though there was very little room in the front seat of the apple-red Corvette, Charlie fell asleep so quickly and so deeply that his hands remained on the steering wheel.

He dreamt of eating breakfast cereal and going to work in an office. He was not unique in this. No one living in Metaphoria has nightmares or even dreams they would describe as 'weird.' Everyone living in Metaphoria dreams in realism. It is one of the few attributes the majority of citizens agree is a positive thing about the city they live in. This is understandable when you realize that a statistically high percentage of the people who find their way to Metaphoria suffer from nightmares back home.

When he finally woke up, Charlie felt incredibly refreshed. As he stretched, he noticed two things: the sun was rising, which cast the shadow of the very top of the Tachycardia Tower across the front door of Forever Yours, and Shirley sat in the passenger seat.

'How's our case going?' Shirley held a purple velvet bag in her lap. Something beat inside it. Charlie checked his watch. He was shocked.

7 HR 23 MIN 11 SEC

'Jesus Christ!'
'What?'
'I just slept for, like, ten hours.'
'Were you dreaming in realism?'
'I was.'

'It's hard to pull yourself from those. Happens all the time here. I once slept for twenty-seven hours dreaming I was stuck in traffic.'

'Jesus! Fuck!'

'I take it our case isn't going that well?'

'No. No, not at all. It's … We're good, actually. I honestly think we're good. What do you know about Forever Yours?'

'Is that why you've parked here? Is Twiggy's heart in there?'

'You've heart of this place?'

'Heard?'

'Have you?'

'Do you value your heart, Charlie?'

'More than ever before.'

This statement was true. The absence of his heart had made Charlie realize not only how much he'd taken it for granted but how much he needed it. He looked at the bag on Shirley's lap. He watched the heart-shaped object move the velvet as it beat, and he knew it was his.

'Do you think your heart's worth more than money?'

'I do now.'

'Well, those who operate and patronize Forever Yours don't agree with you. They treat the human heart as if it were just another commodity, like jewels or stocks. It's a place where men lock their hearts away as if they were just one more thing too valuable to use, something untouchable, precious, as if it were too delicate to withstand the wear and tear of everyday.'

'How do you know it's just men?'

'Isn't that what men want? To live without vulnerability? Without anyone knowing what they're feeling?'

'That's a bit of a generalization.'

'How many female hearts do you think are locked in there, Charlie?'

'Half?'

'It doesn't matter. The whole thing's a scam. The men who rent those vaults believe it because they need it to be true. But just because you remove your heart doesn't stop it from feeling. Sooner or later, one way or another, all that emotion is going to come out. That's the thing about emotion – as long as it stays in the heart, those feelings are indestructible. You can hold it and hold it and hold it, but all that does is build up the pressure. The second it's inevitably released, look out!'

'I was told Twiggy's heart is inside there.'

'That would explain why I can't feel his love for me. Who's your source?'

'It's a good source.'

'It isn't Kitty, is it?'

For the first time, Charlie had doubts about his plan, which temporarily inhibited his ability to speak. He was, however, able to sustain eye contact with Shirley, which is why he noticed that they were turning green.

'I wouldn't put much faith in anything you get from the likes of her.'

'You might want to check out your eyes.'

Shirley twisted the rear-view mirror. She looked at her reflection. She saw that her blue eyes were changing colour. She did not like them this way.

'Do you have a wife?'

'It's complicated.'

'What does that mean?'

'We're not together.'

'Is that why you're here?'

'I think so. Yes.'

'You can't let go?'

'I cannot.'

'And she already has?'

'She's convinced that it's better this way.'

'She no longer believes fighting for the marriage is a path to truth. You should believe her.'

'Why?'

'Because you're here and she's not. There's a good chance that she hasn't been your wife, nor you her husband, for years. I suspect she understands that your describing her relationship to you as wife is a semantic hiccup on your part, a Halloween costume she has stepped out of, leaving you standing there, wearing nothing but an antiquated notion of yourself.' Shirley looked into the rear-view mirror again. She was disappointed to see that her eyes had grown several shades darker green. 'Regardless of all of that, you understand what I'm feeling.'

'Your jealousy is misguided, Shirley.'

'How so?'

'Twiggy's name is not upon her skin.'

Shirley looked from the rear-view mirror to Charlie. Her face softened. For the first time since Charlie had known her – including those eighteen months they'd lived together after university – Shirley's features held a hopeful expression. It was in this moment that Charlie understood how much she loved her husband.

'How can you be sure?' she asked.

'I saw it with my own eyes.'

'Really?'

'Yes.'

'Thank you, Charlie. I wasn't always like this. You remember?'

'You were always a bit intense.'

'Yes. I agree. But I wasn't the sort of person who could cut open an ex-lover's chest and put a bomb in it. What kind of person does something like that?'

'Someone in love.'

'You're trying to be nice?'

'On the contrary. I'm no believer in the idea of tran-scendent love. Love is not some redemptive force. Love inspires the worst in us, not the best. At least it does in me. The cruellest things I've ever done were committed in the effort to try to make someone fall into it with me. Or keep them from falling out of it.'

Shirley raised her hand. Charlie held it. The tenderness in this gesture was the inverse of the cynicism their words expressed.

'We think of love as fairy tales and hugs. When really it's so … '

' … ugly.'

'Desperate.'

'Ruthless.'

'Cutthroat.'

'Animalistic.'

'Carnal.'

'Uncontrollable.'

'Passionate.'

'Powerful.'

'Beautiful.'

'Gorgeous.'

They fell silent. The rest of their thoughts remained unspoken. Charlie opened his pack of Ten Pints and offered one to Shirley. They sat in the front seat puffing out heart-shaped smoke rings. It was at this moment that Charlie felt a pain in the small of his back. Seeking an explanation, he untucked his shirt. Although Charlie could not see his back, his fingers made the discovery for him. There on the small of his back, in a raised cursive font, his fingers made out the words

Shirley Miller

Lost in her own thoughts, Shirley remained unaware that her name had just been written on Charlie's back. She flicked her cigarette out the window, then tossed the velvet bag at Charlie. Charlie watched it beat as it travelled through the air toward him. He caught it with both hands. He pressed it against his chest.

'It was wrong of me to take this in the first place, Charlie.'

'You did it in the name of love.'

'I'm sincerely sorry about the bomb. I'm afraid the only way to disarm it is to solve the case.'

'Or to fail to solve it.'

'That wouldn't be disarming it. That would be detonating it.' Shirley kissed Charlie's cheek. 'If you're asked any question you cannot answer, tell them you were told it would be better not to say.'

'Tell who? When?'

'The people in Forever Yours. I'm assuming you're going in to steal Twiggy's heart?'

'Yes.'

'I doubt that it's there.'

'I'm sure it is.'

'I hope it is. I'm sure my doubts are misguided. Just don't forget that Forever Yours is a confidence scam. Whenever you can't answer one of their questions, act more confident than they are. As if your connections are so powerful their names cannot be mentioned. Since that's exactly what they want to hear, they'll fall for it.'

Shirley got out of his car. At the very moment the passenger door slammed closed, the green light bulb above the front door of Forever Yours turned on. Charlie assumed this meant they were open for business. He carried his heart across the street. The door was large and iron. Charlie stood in front of it, although he did not knock on it. He lifted the purple bag toward the security camera mounted above it.

The camera refocused. His heart beat inside the purple velvet bag. The lock clicked and the heavy door swung open, all on its own.

11

FOREVER YOURS:
A CARDIAC SELF-STORAGE FACILITY

The interior of Forever Yours was impossibly clean. It was overly lit with fluorescent lights. It lacked dust and colour. The walls and the floors were white. Even the carpet that ran from the door into the middle of the room was white. At the end of the carpet sat a desk made of white plastic and sharp right angles. The man sitting behind it appeared dead. He was very pale and slumped backward in a chair in a positon that did not appear sustainable.

Charlie walked toward him. The closer he got to the desk, the more convinced he was that the pale man was dead. He could see that the man's eyes were open, staring up at the ceiling without blinking. The moment Charlie set the purple velvet bag on the desk, the man bolted upright.

'May I help you?' he whispered.

'Can you talk louder?'

'No.'

'Do you want me to whisper?'

'Obviously.'

'I need a place for this,' Charlie whispered. He pointed to the velvet bag on the desk. Together, Charlie and the pale man watched it beat.

'Do you have a reference?'

'Twiggy.'

'Twiggy?'

Thick steel bars shot across the entrance. This door, Charlie now noticed, was the only way in or out of the building. The pale man suppressed most of his smile as he pulled a rotary phone across the desk and began dialling a number from memory. This took some time. There were many digits to dial and most of them appeared to be nines. Charlie stopped counting at seventeen. He waited, patiently, until the pale man's finger finished dialling the very last number and raised the receiver to his ear.

'Let's hope you don't get Kitty,' Charlie whispered.

'Kitty?'

'This morning Shirley discovered what the two of them were calling research. Has he told you about the Spero Machine? It's become a messy situation. It's actually what's prompted me to visit you today.'

The pale man hung up the receiver. Tilting himself forward, he examined Charlie's clothes, the battered shoes, the wrinkles in his jacket, the imprecision with which his tie had been knotted.

'This is how I appeared,' Charlie said.

'This is how *I* appeared.'

'Then you know what I'm talking about.'

'Perhaps even more than you. Perhaps you could describe your association with Mr. Miller?'

'It would be better not to say.'

'Of course.' The pale man ceased to conceal his smile. He clapped his hands three times and a glass staircase descended from the ceiling. With surprisingly nimble steps, he began to climb it, and Charlie followed him up. At the top of the stairs was a small white room that contained two stainless-steel sinks and a large vault door. The pale man took off his jacket, rolled up his sleeves, and scrubbed his hands. Charlie did the same. They dried their hands on thick cotton towels, threw the towels into laundry baskets, then stepped in front of the vault door.

The pale man unfastened the middle three buttons of his shirt. He pressed his chest to a square panel to the right of the vault. The sound of a single heartbeat echoed through the room. Several moments passed before a second followed it. After the third, the red light beside the panel turned green and the vault door began swinging open. The pale man stepped past the door and into a narrow hallway. They were forced to walk in single file. As the door of the vault closed and locked behind them, Charlie's heart, still in the purple velvet bag, began beating faster.

'Twiggy can't recommend this place highly enough. He was quite persuasive, but I'd love to hear your pitch.'

'Pitch?'

'Sell me on your services.'

'There's not much to pitch. We keep your heart safe.'

'So does this velvet bag.'

'Have you not felt a certain objectivity since externalizing your heart?'

'That's … Yes. Exhilarating.' This was a lie. More than objectivity, being away from his heart had provoked a profound despondency, a lack of joy, a significant reduction in Charlie's optimism. While he would admit he also felt an increase in fearlessness, confidence, and self-regard, Charlie did not feel it all balanced out. He was only now realizing the depths his dejection had reached, now that his heart was nearby again. He had never valued his heart more than he did in this very moment.

'Emotion wants to ruin you,' the pale man continued whispering, but since the corridor was narrow and the walls were covered with tin, which reflected sound in unpredictable angles, his voice wasn't just easy to hear but impossible to ignore. 'Emotion wants to take control of your thoughts, your opinions, your decisions. Once you store your heart, you will be free.'

'Your service eliminates emotions?'

'You can no more stop the human heart from generating emotion than you can an anus from excreting waste. But – as I'm sure you've found – the farther away you get from your heart, the less those emotions are felt. The heart will continue to feel, there's nothing anyone can do about that, but putting distance between you and those emotions lessens their impact. Absence makes the heart grow fainter.'

The pale man stopped. The narrow hallway and the tallness of the pale man made it difficult for Charlie to see. Standing on his tiptoes, Charlie was able to glimpse a large steel door that blocked further progress. The pale man began crying. Wiping his tears with his index finger, he made an X on the steel door. It instantly swung open and Charlie followed him inside.

The room was no wider than the hallway but so tall that Charlie was unable to see the ceiling. The walls were covered with thousands of square doors, each one six centimetres wide by eight centimetres tall. A human heart beat behind each one. Thousands of hearts beating behind steel doors. The sound filled the room. It was the most beautiful sound Charlie had ever heard.

'The most favourable box currently unoccupied is #79. Eye level. Respectable neighbours.'

'Sorry? Speak louder.'

'This one. It's for rent.'

'Such a beautiful sound.'

'Yes. Once you store your heart with us, you will be freed of these sorts of impressions as well.'

'Why would I want that?'

'Perhaps some time alone within our vault will convince you. It is a most secure environment. I'll give you just a couple of minutes − #79 won't be unoccupied for long.' Before Charlie could agree or disagree, the pale man shut the thick metal door behind him and Charlie was locked inside the vault. He closed his eyes. He listened intently. The hearts completely drowned out the ticking. It was the first sound to do this. The sound of the hearts gave Charlie his first moments of peace since arriving in Metaphoria. He kept perfectly still for several moments, then found #117.

'You need to open.' Charlie put as much authority into his voice as he could muster.

'Why would I do that?' the lock answered.

'Twiggy's in danger!'

'I think so too!'

'I can save him!'

'I don't think that's true!'

'I can!'

'What's your plan?' the lock said suspiciously.

'To fight them off!'

'Fight who off?'

'They're a powerful organization! They know who you are! They're watching you!'

'Who?'

'The White Blood Cells!'

'Well, if that's who you're worried about, you're too late. They've already been here.'

The keyhole rotated. The lock clicked and the door swung open. Charlie looked inside. Twiggy's heart wasn't there.

12

THE SPERO MACHINE

Confusing what you want for what's meant to be is a very common mistake. It is no stretch to say that Charlie's tendency to do this greatly contributed to why he was stuck in Metaphoria. This was certainly a major factor in why he couldn't let go of his marriage. Charlie felt like he didn't deserve to be the kind of person with a broken marriage, so he believed that getting back together was destined and fated. It didn't matter whether this was something he wanted or not. It was simply something that already existed, a point in the future that, after the right number of days had passed, he'd reach. What Charlie was calling fate was really just hope. And not the good type of hope: it was the dangerous kind generated by denial and the anticipation of things that are unlikely to happen.

His tendency to confuse want and fate was why Charlie was so sure he'd find Twiggy's heart inside Unit #117. That Shirley had sewn a bomb into his chest, leaving him with a literal expiry date, seemed so unfair that Charlie started to believe that finding Twiggy's heart would be easy. When Unit #117 opened and Twiggy's heart wasn't inside, he was devastated. Charlie believed that his faith had failed to be rewarded, when really the problem was that while the idea of fair is something that makes sense to us, the universe is entirely uninterested in the concept.

Unable to admit how afraid this made him, Charlie's fear turned into anger.

'Where's Twiggy's heart?' Charlie yelled at the lock. His voice was so loud and angry that all the hearts began beating faster. The soothing sound of the beating hearts turned into a torrential downpour on a tin roof. But the heart that beat fastest was inside the purple velvet bag.

'Where is Twiggy's heart?'

'I don't know.'

'Where is it?' Charlie grabbed the open door of Unit #117 with both hands. Using all his strength, he pulled downward.

'Don't! Stop it! I'm telling you – I don't know!'

'I'll rip it right off!'

'Please don't!'

'You'll be scrap. Do I not look like a desperate man?'

'Okay. Okay! It was Twiggy!'

'When?'

'Six weeks ago? Not more than seven.'

'Don't lie to me!'

'Stop it! Please! I'm not lying!'

'What about the White Blood Cells?'

'They were here too! But it was after. Twiggy had already taken his heart back.'

'Why? Why did he take it? What was his plan?'

'He didn't say! He didn't say anything! He was alone. He just came and took it. That's all I know. Honest!'

'That's it? He came and took his heart?'

'And left the book!'

'What book?'

'Look inside.'

As Charlie took his hands off the security box, his heart slowed down. The other hearts began beating more slowly as well. Charlie had been so focused on the absence of Twiggy's heart, he'd been unable to see that there was something else inside the security box. Charlie reached in and pulled out a yellow notebook. He opened it and flipped through the pages. He saw complicated diagrams for intricate parts. On the last page was an illustration of the assembled machine, a sprawling mess of tubes and wires and several potted plants. It was labelled:

THE SPERO MACHINE

Charlie slipped the notebook into the inside pocket of his jacket. He slammed shut the door of Unit #117. The hearts stopped beating, the cardiac equivalent of holding their breath, as Charlie walked toward the door of the vault.

'Wait. You can't take that! That's not yours!'

The lock continued to protest. Charlie ignored it. The lock's voice could still be heard as Charlie shut the vault door behind him. He walked down the narrow hallway. He descended the glass staircase. The pale man had returned to his desk. He looked even paler. Once again he was slumped backward in his chair. He bolted upright when Charlie left the last step on the staircase.

'Are you ready to sign?' The pale man stood up, straightened his tie, and brushed the wrinkles from his pants. Nothing he did in any way rectified his rumpled appearance.

'I don't think it's for me.'

'Oh. Okay then.' The iron bars slid away from the entrance. The door opened. The sound of traffic rushed in.

'That's it? No hard sell? You're not going to try and pressure me at all?'

'Oh, you'll be back. Your type always comes back.'

The pale man began to laugh. His laughter echoed off the walls. The sound did not fade. It got louder. The echoes echoed. Soon it sounded like ten pale men were laughing. And then there were hundreds.

Charlie was unable to convince himself that the pale man was wrong. He feared that he had become the kind of man who could do that to his own heart. A part of him suspected he had. Charlie backed through the large open space. He tripped over the white carpet. The pale man laughed harder as Charlie picked himself up, turned himself around, and began running as fast as he could.

13

ZOMBIES AND WINGDINGS

Charlie sat in the driver's seat of the apple-red Corvette. He had not started the engine. His keys remained in his pocket. His eyes were closed. He did not know what to do next. His heart whimpered from inside the purple velvet bag. Charlie wanted to check his watch, but he knew he wasn't currently strong enough for that information to have anything other than a negative effect. He reached into his pocket for his car keys, but his fingers found the walkie-talkie. The channel was already set to Wanda, so he turned it on.

'You there? Over?'

'Yup. Kinda in the middle of a couple of things, though. You okay?'

'I think I'm broken.' Charlie heard Wanda sigh. This was not the sort of support he was looking for. 'What?'

'⚥□◆≈)(■⋎.'

'What?'

'✺◆❷• ᴇ⛏◆◆ ⑤ •♍❷❖♍ ♌♍♍■ □❖♍□ ◆≈)(•,' Wanda said, and then she said nothing. Through the phone, Charlie could hear gunfire in the distance.

'What are you saying? What language are you speaking?'

'✳≈)(•⬧ ℞❖♍□ ☉■⌂ □❖♍□ ☉■⌂ □❖♍□ ◆≈)(•⬧ ♌≈☉□●)(♍⬧ ✺❷❖♍ ᴊ□◆◆☉ ᴊ□⬧ ✺❷○ □♍ ☉●●◺)(■ ◆≈♍ ○)(⌂⌂●♍ □⤢ •□□♍◆≈)(■ᴊ⬧◐.'

'This is so frustrating.'

'That's how I feel.'

'No. It's not that. What were you saying?'

'Seriously? You want me to say it again?'

'Please?'

'Do you still love your kids?'

'What kind of question is that?'

'So you do?'

'Of course.'

'⬛ ⬥〜⬙ ●⬜•• ⬜⤢ ⊠⬜⬥⬜ ●⬜✦〜 ⤢⬜⬜ ⊠⬜⬥⬜ •⊁⤢〜 〜⊙•■⬤⬥ ♍〜⊙■⬙♍♎ ⬥〜〜 ●⬜✦〜 ⊠⬜⬥ 〜⊙✦〜 ⤢⬜⬜ ⊠⬜⬥⬜ &⟩⬥⬙•?'

'Wait … '

'✳〜〜■ ℰ✦•✦ ♎⬜ ⟩✦✎ ☝⬜■⬤✦ 〜✦〜■ ⊙■••〜⬜ → ◖●⬜•〜 ⊠⬜⬥⬜ 〜⊠〜• ⊙■♎ ⤢〜〜● ⬥〜〜 ●⬜✦ 〜 ⊠⬜⬥ 〜⊙✦〜 ⤢⬜⬜ ⊠⬜⬥⬜ &⟩⬥⬙•.'

'You're doing it again! Or it's happening again.'

'What is?'

'What were you just saying?'

'✳〜〜■ ℰ✦•✦ ♎⬜ ⟩✦✎ ☝⬜■⬤✦ 〜✦〜■ ⊙■••〜⬜ ⬯ ◖●⬜•〜 ⊠⬜⬥⬜ 〜⊠〜• …'

'No, not the content. What were you talking about?'

'We could talk on and on and on about it. We already have. But it's not about me having the answers. You have to figure it out. For yourself.'

'That's what you were saying?'

'No, I was telling you to ♑〜✦ ⊠⬜⬥⬜ ⤢✦♍&⟩■♑ •〜⟩✦ ✦⬜♑〜✦〜⬜⬯ ✳〜⬤✦ ⊠⬜✦ ♎⬜■⬤✦ ⬜〜⬤••⊠ ●⬜✦〜 〜〜⬜ ⊙■◯⬜⬜〜⬯ ✳〜⬤✦ ⊠⬜✦ ⤢〜〜● ♑✦⟩✦✦⊠ ⊙♌⬜✦✦ ■⬜✦ ●⬜✦⟩■♑ 〜〜⬜ ⊙■◯⬜⬜〜⬰ ✦〜⬤✦ ⊠⬜✦'

⸻

'I didn't –'

'And that isn't holding just you back: it's holding us back.'

'How come the part where you scold me comes through?' Charlie knew Wanda was right, even though he hadn't understood most of what she'd said. Something that Metaphoria was doing was finally making sense to Charlie.

'I have to go. I'm literally fighting off zombies.'

'Jesus.'

'They all look like my college boyfriend. It's fucked up, Charlie.'

The gunfire got louder and closer and then the signal from the walkie-talkie turned into static.

14

HEART COMPASS

It wasn't just the ticking, or how afraid he was to look at his watch, or that Twiggy's heart hadn't been in Unit #117, leaving him with no leads and no suspects — it was the sound of the Cyclops's wedding ring dragging behind the apple-red Corvette that pushed Charlie too far. The squeal of the ring against the pavement, a sound that made manifest both the impractical pureness of the gold and the compulsive utility of the pavement, objects that when forced to collide produced a shriek that sounded exactly like love going bad, triggered his shrinking.

At first Charlie thought the steering wheel was getting bigger, but soon he was unable to reach the pedals and his sightline sunk below the dashboard. He momentarily attempted to believe that the whole car was getting bigger, but then his watch slid down his arm and he couldn't deny the truth. No longer able to reach either pedal nor strong enough to control the steering wheel, Charlie feared that the car might crash. This was an unnecessary fear: weighted down by the Cyclops's wedding ring, the car coasted to a stop almost immediately.

Charlie was shrinking much faster than he had in his office. His head slipped through the collar of his still-buttoned shirt. He looked up and saw the cotton fabric sailing down toward him like a parachute. It covered him completely and he struggled to crawl through the space between two buttons. He continued to shrink. There seemed no way to stop it. Charlie Waterfield became resigned to his fate. It was better, or at least more peaceful, than having his body blown apart by the bomb.

It was at this point that Charlie heard static coming from the walkie-talkie. It was impossible to ignore. The speaker was three times larger than he was. The sound it produced was almost deafening, although still not as loud as the ticking in his ears. He tried to ignore it but found that he couldn't. Then his ex-wife's voice came through and Charlie gave it the whole of his attention.

'Charlie?'

Charlie struggled through the space between the third and fourth button of his shirt. With a running start, he leapt from the driver's seat onto the passenger seat. The walkie-talkie lay on its side. Charlie climbed up. He jumped onto the call button and, using all of his weight, managed to depress it.

'I'm here! I'm here!'

'You sound far away. It's a bad connection.'

'You sound great. There's something I need to tell you.'

'Is it about camp? Because I went ahead and booked the two weeks in August. You said that will work.'

'No, it's not about camp.'

'Good. So that works?'

'Yeah. It's good. But what I need to say to you – '

'Mark wants to say hello.'

'Okay. But first, let me tell you – '

'Dad?'

'Hey, man! Oh my god! It's so great to hear you.' Charlie looked up at the purple velvet bag, which sat on the passenger seat beside the walkie-talkie. It looked to be two storeys high. At the sound of his son's voice, his heart had begun beating faster and faster. Charlie watched the velvet fabric move in and out. He failed to notice that his rate of shrinking had not only slowed, but stopped.

'Can you give me the password?'

'For what?'

'The iTunes password.'

'Why?'

'There's a game I want to buy.'

'Is it violent?'

'Not really.'

'How not really?'

'It is. But there's a creative mode too. You can totally make stuff in creative mode. And I really want to get it. Jake and I, we're going to make a golf course.'

'Why a golf course?'

'Because there are golf carts.'

'How much is it?' Charlie asked, but he had already decided to let the kid have it. At this moment, under these circumstances, building a virtual golf course seemed like the most rational, logical thing he'd ever heard. Charlie looked up. He watched the purple velvet bag get smaller and smaller.

'It's twenty bucks.'

'What?'

'I can pay half.'

'You can pay all of it.'

'I will! Then I can get it?'

'Sure. It's FloatHopes100.' Charlie picked up the purple velvet bag and set it in his lap. Then he held the walkie-talkie close to his mouth. 'How come you can never remember that?'

'Capital F, capital H?'

'Yes.'

'Don't forget I have karate.'

'I haven't.'

Having returned to his full size, Charlie sat naked in the passenger seat of his car. He dressed slowly. Feeling a sudden affection for his heart, Charlie tipped it out of the velvet purple bag and set it on the dashboard. He returned to the driver's seat, started the engine, and if it's possible to take random turns in Metaphoria, Charlie took them.

Seven rights and four lefts later, Charlie noticed something quite interesting about his heart, or more specifically his superior vena cava. No matter which way he turned, his superior vena cava pointed in the same direction. Charlie took lefts and rights as his heart directed him, using his superior vena cava as the needle in a compass.

Thirty-five minutes in, Charlie began having doubts that this navigational technique was sound. He thought about how much time he was losing. The belief that his heart could actually lead him somewhere useful and important seemed naive and romantic and useless. Still, some part of him urged him to persist, so, having few other options, he did. He continued following whatever direction his superior vena cave pointed to for forty minutes, and then fifty. He'd pretty much given up all belief that he was doing anything but wasting extremely valuable time when, just after an hour of this, he arrived at the Library of Blank Pages.

15

THE LIBRARY OF BLANK PAGES

Charlie patted down his hair, straightened his tie, and attempted to push the wrinkles out of his suit with his hand. The more he did this, the messier his hair and the more rumpled his clothes became. Since he was in Metaphoria, Charlie was forced to accept that further grooming would be equally ineffective – he would look a mess in front of Wanda because he was one.

The frosted glass door to the Library of Blank Pages opened easily. Inside there were high ceilings, long tables, and empty shelves. Charlie saw books everywhere: standing in stacks, pushed into giant piles that reached the ceiling, a metre deep on the floor. And on top of the books were numerous zombie corpses. With great effort, Charlie waded through it all.

'Wanda?'

'Up here! By the microfiche!'

The stairs were book-laden and difficult to climb. When he reached the second floor, he saw Wanda leaning against a long wooden reading table, dressed in a uniform from the British army, circa 1942. A small puff of heart-shaped smoke drifted from the barrel of her machine gun. Her hair was dishevelled and her clothes wrinkled. She looked a mess, because she was one. They waded through books toward each other, but when they met, a strange and telling problem arose. As she opened her arms and Charlie tried to hug her, his body went right through her. Charlie was unable to touch any part of Wanda's body with any part of his.

'That's … '

' … weird.'

'Is it metaphoric?'

'Are you thinking about Linda?'

'Why would you even ask that?'

'Are you?'

'No.'

'That just makes it worse.'

'How do you know it's not *you*?'

'Because I can touch you.' To prove it, Wanda put her left hand gently on Charlie's cheek. He closed his eyes. His heart beat faster, which attracted Wanda's attention.

'What's in the bag?' she asked.

'My heart.'

'Good one.'

Charlie upended the purple velvet bag onto the long wooden reading table. His superior vena cava pointed directly at Wanda in a way that was almost rude. Charlie's heart jumped off the table and into Wanda's arms. She cradled it, petting the aorta like she would the head of a dog.

'Oh my god! Your heart is so ugly it's adorable!'

'Thank you?'

'At least your heart can touch me.'

'That seems metaphoric too.' Charlie's heart nestled into the crook of her arm.

'How long have you been here?'

'It was right after I left your house. There was a guy in the back of my car — '

'Purple hat?'

'Yes.'

'British accent?'

'Posh.'

'Kept talking about this magical city, Metaphoria?'

'Exactly.'

'Smell of burnt cedar – '

' – and purple smoke. And the next thing I knew, I woke up in the Epiphany Detective Agency. How did you get here?'

'After you left, I ordered dumplings.'

'Comfort food.'

'Sounds like my delivery man was the same person you met in the back of the cab. Says he doesn't need a tip if I listen to him describe the city of Metaphoria. Next thing I know ... poof! I woke up in the Library of Blank Pages.'

'Why are all the books on the ground?'

'Well, that's an interesting story. At first, no one ever came here because all the books were blank. It was nothing but a library of books that had never been written. But then one day, a forty-seven-year-old forensic accountant named Maciek Guy stepped inside. It was his sixth day in Metaphoria. Overwhelmed by seeing his problems stitched into the fabric of the everyday, he ran inside the Library of Blank Pages to seek relief. He liked the fact that the books were blank. The complete lack of narrative felt soothing. He sat in the relative metaphoric silence for quite some time before curiosity got the better of him. Maciek approached the shelves. He plucked a thick red leather-bound book from an upper shelf. He chose the book randomly. He opened it randomly. And what appeared on the page was this ... '

Wanda looked down at the ground. She pulled a book from the floor. She opened it randomly. She nodded her head, then turned the book so that Charlie could see it. There were only three words printed on that page:

Yes, she does.

Keeping the book turned toward Charlie, Wanda closed it, then opened it again. She had opened the book at random and yet the same phrase was printed on the page. She did this three more times. Each time she did, those same three words were all that was printed there.

'Maciek flipped through the book. To his great surprise, that phrase appeared on every page. This would not have had any significance had Maciek not been wondering whether his wife still loved him at the exact moment he'd pulled the book off the shelf. He flipped through the pages a second time, confirming that the same phrase was repeated over and over again. He became convinced that his wife did in fact love him, that the book was telling him the truth. He ran to the nearest payphone and called his wife. He told her that he loved her. She said she loved him too.'

'Did he poof?'

'He did.'

'Lucky bastard.'

'Right? So you can imagine how quickly word got around. That there was a library of books that would answer, truthfully, any question posed to them. The Library of Blank Pages was the talk of Metaphoria! Crowds stormed the library. Soon the shelves were empty. Every book had been asked a question, and the book had given the answer, which appeared on every page inside it.

'Now there isn't a blank book left in the Library of Blank Pages. The books lie scattered across the floor, clumped into piles. And if you go through them, only four answers appear across all of these pages ... '

Wanda dug through the books at her feet. She opened and closed several, eventually selecting four. These four books she opened and put side by side on the long wooden reading table. On the pages of each book there was a single phrase. Each of the four phrases was only slightly different:

Yes, he does.

No, he doesn't.

Yes, she does.

No, she doesn't.

'Such a goddamn waste.' Using her arm and considerable force, Wanda swept all four books off the table. The books, travelling spine up, flapped several times as they flew across the room. 'From the infinite number of questions that could have been asked, the untold knowledge that the Library of Blank Pages could have provided, the very secrets of the universe it could have revealed – the only question humanity asked was "Do they still love me?"'

'The desire for love makes all of us weak.'

'Is your life in danger?'

'I have less than twenty-four hours to find Twiggy Miller's missing heart or I will explode. How about you?'

'A sinister organization bent on world domination has kidnapped David Templeman, and is using him to create an army of zombie clones. Their first mission is to kill me.'

'Who is David Templeman?'

'That's your first question?'

'The desire for love makes all of us weak.'

'We lived together in university. I haven't seen him in years.'

'Do you still love him?'

'I love the idea of him.'

'It still doesn't explain why I just found out about your husband.'

'Proximity doesn't make a husband, Charlie. Just because we share the same house doesn't mean we're intimate.'

'That's easy to say.'

'What do you want me to say?'

'Explain why you lied to me!'

'I was selfish, Charlie. I know it. But I didn't try to fall in love with you. I tried very hard not to. And then when I did, I just didn't want to lose you.'

'So none of this is your fault?'

'Don't do that. Don't turn me into a cliché, some sort of femme fatale with paranormal control over your feelings. I didn't manipulate you. Why would I? Do you know how complicated falling in love with you has made my life?'

'Then why didn't you just leave him?'

'If I could answer that question, I'd know the purpose of the human heart.'

'True enough.'

'I'm fucked up, Charlie. But so you are. That's why we're here.'

'But not telling me about the fact that you're married? That's huge. That's messed up.'

'Kiss me.'

Charlie couldn't refuse. He leaned close. He tried to kiss Wanda, but his lips touched nothing but air.

'See? You're not exactly without your own contribution to our fucked-up romance.' Wanda swung the machine gun over her shoulder, pushed off from the table, and began walking away. She waded through the books. The elevator arrived at the exact moment she reached it. Wanda got inside. The doors closed.

All Charlie could do was watch the elevator take her away.

16

RETURN OF THE CYCLOPS

It was raining sheet music when Charlie came out of the Library of Blank Pages. Crisp white scores, lined with staffs and dotted with notes, fell through the air. Each page struck a note as it hit the ground, producing random plunks, a Cage-like cat pacing the length of a piano. Charlie didn't try to figure out what it meant. He allowed himself to become engrossed in the beauty of it. That is why he didn't notice how quickly the Cyclops was approaching him.

'You said you were going to stay away from her!'

'I think I love her!'

'You think?'

The Cyclops punched Charlie in the face. The punch knocked him off his feet and into the air. His bottom lip split open. He spat out a tooth. He continued to rise. The pain was intense but the view was amazing. Charlie saw the tops of trees. He got a brief glimpse of Wanda working in the west turret of the Library of Blank Pages. Soon the Tachycardia Tower was the only thing higher than he was. Having reached his zenith, Charlie hovered in the air, going neither up nor down, and it was at this exact moment that the Unnamed Ghost returned.

'Have you figured me out?'

'I've been a little busy,' Charlie said, his nose filled with the smell of oranges drifting off the Ghost.

'You have to take this seriously!' The Unnamed Ghost rattled his glowing chains.

'Does it look like I'm enjoying myself?'

The Ghost took a good look at Charlie. He saw the missing tooth, the bloodied lip, the vigorous pace with which his heart beat inside the velvet bag.

'No, it doesn't. But there's something wrong. You're holding on to something. I suspect it's hope.'

'Why does everyone keep talking about hope?'

Charlie wanted to ask more, but gravity reasserted itself. He could only watch as the Unnamed Ghost faded away. The closer Charlie got to the ground, the faster he fell. He fell through the sheet music without making a sound. He had no way of stopping. Flipping himself around, Charlie pointed his head at the ground. He reasoned that this would make it faster. Just as Charlie's hair brushed the concrete sidewalk, the Cyclops caught him.

'Why did you save me?'

'Because I want you to suffer.'

The Cyclops ripped the purple velvet bag from Charlie's hand. He dumped Charlie's heart into his giant hand. Together, they watched it beat. The Cyclops smiled, although this smile was unfriendly. He turned his palm over and let Charlie's heart fall toward the ground. The Cyclops pulled his foot swiftly back, swung it quickly forward, and kicked Charlie's heart.

Charlie's heart went like this:

t

r

a

e

h

17

THE SPERO MACHINE, SWITCHED ON

Charlie Waterfield's heart ascended into the sky. Charlie ran underneath it. He ran as fast as he could, which was hard to do with a bomb where his heart should be. When Charlie's heart reached its zenith, it hovered in the sky. Charlie stopped directly beneath it, trying to catch his breath. With his hands on his knees, he looked up at his heart. It was directly in front of the sun. Charlie's own heart cast a heart-shaped shadow over him. Then it began to fall.

The closer Charlie's heart got to the ground, the faster it fell, and the faster Charlie ran. He ran with his arms outstretched. His eyes remained on his heart. Cars swerved around him as he ran down the middle of the street. His heart fell faster. It came closer to the ground. Charlie dived headfirst through the air. His fingers caught his heart centimetres above the sidewalk.

Charlie's heart was happy to see him. It beat quickly. It had sustained a small crack near the right ventricle, but otherwise looked no worse than when Shirley first took it out of his chest. Charlie patted it gently. His heart pushed its right auricle against Charlie's hand. Charlie put his heart in the breast pocket of his jacket. His right and left carotid branches, subclavian branches, and innominate artery stuck out of the top like a pocket square. As the ventricles expanded and collapsed, they moved the fabric of his jacket pocket.

Charlie stood in front of an art deco movie theatre. The marquee proclaimed it to be the Kummerspeck Theatre. He wondered what part of Metaphoria he was in. Hearing a commotion behind him, Charlie, who was still standing in the middle of the street, turned around. Rushing down the street toward him was a vast collection of citizens, a roaring crowd that moved as one thing, like a flock of starlings.

They were all headed for the Kummerspeck. There were so many people, and they were moving so quickly, that Charlie got caught up in this wave of humanity. He was swept into the Kummerspeck. The crowd pushed him past the concession stand, into the theatre, down the centre aisle. Losing his balance, Charlie tumbled into an empty seat.

Although the crowd was in an extreme rush, the show did not start the moment everyone was seated. The house lights remained on. Charlie was free to leave, but some part of him made him stay. The wait seemed very, very long. And all through it, not a single member of the audience spoke, or coughed, or even fidgeted in their seat. Charlie looked at his watch.

3 HR 57 MIN 16 SEC

This meant he'd spent nearly an hour waiting for the show to begin. He decided he would not throw more good minutes after bad. But just as he was about to stand, the house lights dimmed.

The curtains parted. A blue spotlight shone on the middle of the stage. The crowd stood but remained eerily silent. Twiggy stepped into the spotlight. He wore a rumpled white lab coat. The arms of his shirt and jacket had been removed, revealing his sticks. His smile was open and encouraging. His hair was a mess and stuck up from the top of his head in various directions. He leaned close to the microphone but didn't speak. The audience did not make a sound. Popcorn could be heard popping in the concession stand.

Twiggy held this silence. No one moved. Several of the people around Charlie were holding their breath.

'Who wants to know if their love is true?' Twiggy asked quietly.

The crowd screamed. The sound drowned out the ticking. Charlie stood. He did this because he was the only one in the theatre who hadn't and he felt a sudden need to be inconspicuous. He had never seen a crowd this worked up before. And then, as Twiggy took two steps backward and pulled a black velvet cloth off a long wooden table, everyone became completely, instantly silent again.

Everyone, including Twiggy, stared at the complicated machine that sat in the middle of the wooden table. The device was a mess of wires and tubes and several potted plants. Charlie recognized it from the back page of the yellow notebook he'd taken from Unit #117 of Forever Yours.

'I give you the Spero Machine!' Twiggy stepped toward it. The crowd remained still and silent. Twiggy put his finger underneath a large silver switch. Several people in the audience gasped. 'I almost forgot! How could I be so absent-minded? The Spero Machine will need a source of power! How could I forget my own heart?'

The blue spotlight turned bright white. It shone on Twiggy as he unbuttoned his shirt. There, in the middle of his chest, was a rectangular door. His twig fingers opened it. Inside glowed an orange heart. In that moment, Twiggy's heart was the most beautiful thing Charlie had ever seen. Using long silver wires, Twiggy connected his heart to the Spero Machine.

'Now we're ready.' Twiggy flicked the switch. The Spero Machine began to emit a deep low-frequency hum. The windowpanes rattled. The sound slowly got louder. 'Who wants to be first?'

Everyone in the crowd called out to be chosen. Charlie did as well. He raised his hand higher. He jumped up and down, hoping to attract Twiggy's attention.

It was at this point that Charlie felt the unmistakable pressure of a circular piece of metal push into his back and, although this had never happened to him before, he knew without a doubt that he was at gunpoint.

18

ATTACK OF THE WHITE BLOOD CELLS

Charlie raised his hands, turned around, and saw a tall, thin woman dressed in medical scrubs, whom he vaguely remembered but couldn't place. He felt as if his attachment to her was of vital importance, so his failure to remember how he knew her disturbed him profoundly.

That this was the first time in his life he'd ever had a gun pointed at him played into his unease as well.

'You don't recognize me, do you?'

'Maybe it's the scrubs?'

'My name is Scarlett Royale. I used to have your job.'

'Which job?'

'Didn't you check the wall? In your office?'

'The pictures?'

'I'm third from the right, second row.'

'But that's not how we know each other. Right?'

'I used to have your job. The sole detective of the Epiphany Detective Agency.'

'Did you like it?'

'How are *you* enjoying the position?'

'I'm not sure I'm very good at it. I've never wanted to be a detective. To be honest, I've never been that intrigued by mysteries in general.'

'I think that's the point.'

'What? That I fail?'

'That you become intrigued by mystery and start looking for solutions.'

'Let's start with why you're pointing a gun at me.'

'See? You're getting it. I want Twiggy's heart. Just give it to me and the gun goes away.'

'It's right up there!' Charlie pointed to the stage.

The audience had begun forming a single line, with Twiggy at the head. His shirt and heart-door were still open. The spotlight bounced off his glowing orange heart.

'Hate to break it to you, Chuck, but even in Metaphoria no one's heart is that beautiful. Especially not Twiggy Miller's.'

This rang true. Keeping his arms raised and his toes pointed toward the woman, Charlie twisted his upper body to take a good look at Twiggy's glowing heart.

'Look closely,' Scarlett said. 'You'll see that the glow flickers. Now look at the stage. It's hard to make out, but there's an electrical cord that runs across the stage and up Twiggy's left pant leg. His glowing heart is a fake.'

'Why do you think *I* have the real thing?'

'We saw the security tape from Forever Yours. We know you were the last one into the vault.'

'Who's we?'

'The White Blood Cells.'

'I have to ask: are you guys racists?'

'We're not a racist organization! White Blood Cells, like in the body. Leukocytes that live in the blood and lymphatic system that protect the body from infections and foreign bodies. Just like white blood cells protect the body, we are dedicated to the preservation of love.'

'Still, it's coming off racist.'

'Everybody says that.'

Charlie didn't know what else to say. They both felt slightly ridiculous, Scarlett for holding the gun, Charlie for having a gun held on him. The longer they failed to say anything more, the larger their sense of ridiculousness grew. So it was a relief to both of them when a bell began to ring and the crowd suddenly doubled its enthusiasm. Onstage an indicator light on the front of the Spero Machine began flashing green. Triumphant orchestral music burst through the speakers and hot pink balloons rained down from the ceiling.

'We have true love!' Twiggy's voice boomed through the room.

'Perhaps we could talk away from the circus.' Scarlett kept the gun against the small of Charlie's back. She directed him through the crowd. The walkie-talkie was in his pocket and he could hear Wanda calling him, but he didn't dare reach for it. The barrel rubbed against a tender patch of skin at the small of his back. Charlie realized he was still sore from the appearance of Shirley's name. Outside, an idling ambulance waited at the curb. Red and blue lights flashed. The woman opened the back doors of the ambulance and pushed Charlie inside, then climbed in after him. She closed the doors behind her and plucked Charlie's heart from the breast pocket of his jacket.

'That's not Twiggy's. That's mine.'

'I wouldn't have it any other way.'

The ambulance pulled away from the curb. Charlie couldn't see who was driving. He kept his hands raised. With surprising dexterity, the woman flipped the gun into the air, caught it by the barrel, then used the butt to strike Charlie's head, rendering him unconscious.

19

THE HEART'S INTERROGATION

Charlie woke up in the back of an ambulance, which made him feel cared for. Sensing the vehicle's forward motion, Charlie assumed he was being rushed to the hospital. He remembered being abducted by gunpoint and struck on the head by the butt of a gun and was thankful to be getting the medical treatment he required. But these feelings of goodwill evaporated instantly when he realized that the person riding with him in the back of the ambulance was Scarlett Royale, the same person who'd done those things to him.

'Finally. Now that you're awake, we can start. I want you to see this.'

'How long have I been out for?'

'Ninety-three minutes.'

'Jesus. I hope these concussions are metaphoric.'

Scarlett Royale's left hand held both the gun and Charlie's heart. With her right she pulled a worn leather suitcase from underneath the gurney. The suitcase did not, in any way, look medical.

'Capitalism, to serve its own purpose, has made us believe we're helpless to create our own happiness. Do you know how it's done this?' Scarlett opened the clasps on the suitcase one at a time.

'By putting a price on it?'

'Exactly, Mr. Waterfield. Impressive. Capitalism has co-opted our emotions.' She opened the suitcase. Dust went everywhere. Inside were several pieces of clock-like machinery. 'Capitalism has taken control of our hate and fear – but what governmental, political, or religious organization hasn't used those to keep control of the population? There is nothing new about that. No, what late-period capitalism is doing is far more sinister. It's taken control of the emotions we cherish the most: love and hope. It's used our natural capacity to hope to make us crave something unattainable, and then, through the use of advertising, convinced us that thing is love. The consequences of this being nothing less than that, for the first time in humanity, love – or at least what the vast majority of people have been brainwashed into believing is love –is no longer free.

'Do you know Morse code, Mr. Waterfield?'

'No.'

'Excellent.'

A long coiled cord, the type of thing that used to connect the handset to the body of a telephone, attached the suitcase to a device that resembled a stethoscope. Only, where the ends of a regular stethoscope would have been flat, there were three rows of sharpened metal teeth. Charlie saw his heart recoil from where it sat on the purple velvet bag.

'It's going to hurt just a little bit.'

Scarlett Royale was lying to Charlie Waterfield. When she fastened the end of the Morse machine to Charlie's left and right ventricles, it hurt quite a bit more than just a little bit. Even though his heart was half an ambulance length away, the pain Charlie felt was intense. His fingers curled. He screamed. Long, thin lines of blood squirted from Charlie's heart.

'What does that have to do with Twiggy's heart?'

'We know Twiggy's at the centre of something evil. We know you have his heart. We saw the tape of you leaving Forever Yours. We just don't know where you've stashed it. Or what Twiggy's ultimate agenda is. Or, more importantly to me, how the Epiphany Detective Agency is connected to it. But that really isn't a problem for us. Because one of the main tenets of the White Blood Cells is a belief that while the mouth lies, the heart never does. That's why we've decided to talk to it directly.'

Scarlett kept her pistol trained on Charlie as she adjusted various dials and switches. Whatever she was doing, it required trial and error. A high-pitched static, like a short-wave radio produces, became louder and then softer and then faded away.

'We are the White Blood Cells. Have you heard of us?'

'You just explained that … '

'I wasn't talking to you'

'♥♥ / ♥♥♥.'

The sound of Charlie's heart came through a speaker in the base of the suitcase. It beat in long and short thubs. Scarlett leaned close to Charlie's heart. She patted the subclavian branches gently.

'That's okay. But you need to trust me. I know that you're scared, but we need to talk. We are an organization dedicated to ensuring that the wisdom of the heart is allowed full expression. So, I ask this question with the greatest seriousness: where is Twiggy's heart?'

'♥♥♥ / ♥♥ / ♥♥♥ / ♥♥ ' ♥ … ♥♥ / ♥ … ♥ / ♥♥ … ♥♥♥♥ /
♥♥ / ♥♥♥ … ♥♥♥♥ / ♥♥♥♥ / ♥ / ♥♥♥ / ♥?'

'No. That was a fake. It wasn't Twiggy's real heart, just a prop, a piece of the theatre that Twiggy was performing.'

'♥♥ … ♥ / ♥♥♥♥ / ♥♥ / ♥♥ / ♥♥♥ … ♥♥♥♥ / ♥♥♥ /
♥♥♥' ♥♥♥ / ♥ … ♥♥♥ / ♥♥♥ / ♥♥♥ / ♥♥ / ♥♥♥ … ♥♥ /
♥♥♥♥ / ♥♥♥ / ♥♥♥ / ♥ … ♥ / ♥♥♥♥ / ♥♥ / ♥♥♥♥♥ / ♥♥♥
/ ♥♥♥ … ♥♥♥♥ / ♥♥ / ♥♥♥♥ / ♥ … ♥ / ♥♥♥ … ♥♥♥♥ /
♥♥♥ / ♥♥♥ / ♥♥♥ … ♥♥♥♥ / ♥♥♥♥ / ♥♥♥ / ♥♥♥ / ♥ /
♥♥♥.'

'It was a pretty good fake, admittedly, but it wasn't his real heart. But tell me – doesn't Charlie know where Twiggy's heart is?'

'♥♥♥♥ / ♥♥♥ / ♥♥♥ … ♥♥♥ / ♥♥♥ / ♥♥♥ / ♥♥♥♥ / ♥♥♥
… ♥♥♥♥ / ♥ … ♥♥♥ / ♥♥ / ♥♥♥ / ♥♥♥ … ♥♥ / ♥♥♥♥ … ♥♥
… ♥♥♥ / ♥♥♥ / ♥♥ ' ♥?'

'You'd be surprised what men try to hide from their hearts.'

'♥♥♥♥ / ♥♥♥♥ / ♥♥ / ♥♥♥ / ♥♥♥♥ / ♥♥ / ♥ … ♥♥ / ♥♥♥ …
♥♥ … ♥♥♥ / ♥♥♥ / ♥♥♥ / ♥♥♥ … ♥♥ / ♥♥ / ♥♥.'

'Then why is he in Metaphoria?'

'♥♥♥ / ♥♥♥♥ / ♥♥♥♥ … ♥♥ / ♥♥♥ /♥ … ♥♥♥♥ / ♥♥♥
/ ♥♥♥ … ♥♥ / ♥♥ … ♥♥ / ♥ / ♥ / ♥♥ / ♥♥♥♥ / ♥♥♥♥ / ♥♥♥
/ ♥♥♥ / ♥♥ / ♥♥?'

'True enough. I'm here too. But at least I'm fighting on the side of good. Our operatives saw Waterfield leaving Forever Yours with Twiggy's heart in a purple velvet bag.'

'♥ / ♥♥♥♥ / ♥♥ / ♥ … ♥♥♥ / ♥♥ / ♥♥♥ / ♥♥ ' ♥ … ♥ /
♥♥♥ / ♥♥ / ♥♥♥ / ♥♥♥ / ♥♥♥♥ ' ♥♥♥ … ♥♥♥♥ / ♥ / ♥♥ /
♥♥♥ / ♥. ♥♥ / ♥ … ♥♥♥ / ♥♥ / ♥♥♥ … ♥♥ / ♥.'

'Are you sure it was you?'

'♥♥ … ♥ / ♥♥♥♥ / ♥♥♥ / ♥♥♥ / ♥♥♥ / ♥♥♥♥ / ♥ … ♥ /
♥♥♥♥ / ♥♥ / ♥ … ♥ / ♥♥♥♥ / ♥ … ♥♥♥♥ / ♥ / ♥♥ / ♥♥♥ / ♥
… ♥♥ / ♥♥♥♥ / ♥♥♥ / ♥♥ / ♥♥♥♥ / ♥♥♥ … ♥ / ♥♥♥ /
♥♥♥♥ / ♥♥♥ … ♥ / ♥♥♥♥ / ♥ … ♥ / ♥♥♥ / ♥♥♥ / ♥ / ♥♥♥♥?'

'How is he connected to the Sarzanello Project?'

'What's the Sarzanello Project?' Charlie asked.

'Shut up, Waterfield! No one's asking you!'

'♥♥♥ / ♥♥♥ / ♥♥ ' ♥ … ♥ / ♥♥ / ♥♥♥♥ / ♥♥♥ … ♥ /
♥♥♥ … ♥♥♥♥ / ♥♥ / ♥♥ …♥♥♥♥ / ♥♥ / ♥♥♥ / ♥ … ♥ /
♥♥♥♥ / ♥♥ / ♥!'

'I will talk to him any way I want to!'

'♥♥♥♥ / ♥♥♥ / ♥♥♥♥ / ♥♥♥ … ♥♥♥♥ / ♥♥♥ / ♥♥♥!'

'What is the Sarzanello Project?'

'♥♥♥♥ / ♥♥♥ / ♥♥♥♥ / ♥♥♥ … ♥♥♥♥ / ♥♥♥ / ♥♥♥!'

'As goes the man, so goes the heart.' Scarlett unhooked Charlie's heart from the Morse machine, wound up the cables, and unplugged it. 'It pains me to see a heart so loyal to a fool.'

'Why did you say that? Tell me what my heart is saying!'

Scarlett opened the back doors of the ambulance and then her arms. Charlie, confused but sincerely in need of affection, embraced her. The hug was the second nicest thing that had happened to him since arriving in Metaphoria. Charlie closed his eyes. He leaned into her body. She held him tightly. Then she twirled around, so that Charlie's back was to the open doors, and pushed him out of the ambulance.

'But I have to get my son to karate,' Charlie said as he drifted through the air. He hit the pavement with significant force and tumbled down the middle of the road. When his momentum was finally spent, he sat up and spit out a tooth. He was bleeding from several locations. Looking east, Charlie saw the ambulance recede into the distance. Scarlett waved from the back.

'I do this for love,' she yelled. She held Charlie's heart. They both watched Charlie's heart beat. Then she let it fall, pulled back her leg, and kicked.

Charlie's heart went like this:

t

r

a

e

h

20

THE WISDOM OF POE TEXTERMAN

Charlie watched his heart go higher and higher. His faith was attached to it; the higher his heart went, the farther away his faith was. At first he lost faith in beneficial yet unproven notions, like gravity, the benefits of compassion, that things have a way of working themselves out. Which was why Charlie felt that running after his heart wasn't worth the effort. As his heart continued its ascent, Charlie lost his faith in humanity. And as his heart became a black dot in the sky, then got so small he could no longer see it, he lost faith in himself. He sank to his knees in the middle of the street, stopping traffic in both directions.

One of the drivers affected by Charlie's collapse was Poe Textermen. A tall, thin man with the head of a raven, Poe was driving a van for the Sarzanello Moving Company and was running late. He was also one of only twenty-six people to ever have been born in Metaphoria. Poe wasn't trying to trigger a poof. Metaphoria was his home. Poe knew Metaphoria better than anyone else. His car was directly in front of Charlie. Having seen this situation before, Poe got out of his car and leaned against the hood. He gave Charlie what he considered enough time, and then he spoke.

'Hey, buddy. Everybody breaks down, but you can't do it in the middle of the street,' Poe said.

Charlie didn't move. At this moment his entire belief system was unravelling like a poorly knit acrylic sweater.

His belief in even simple things, like that he had a right to continue existing, or an ability to heal himself, was so tenuous that even certain phrases would have shattered him into pieces too small to mend. Had Poe shouted at Charlie and demanded he move, he would have further lost his faith in humanity, which would have destroyed him. Had Poe thrown out a solution, suggesting that Charlie's problem was so trivial it could be cured by casual words tossed out by a stranger, he would have begun shrinking so quickly that anyone watching would have assumed he'd disappeared.

Poe's response did something quite different, which produced a completely unexpected result. The absence of heavy-handed compassion made Charlie feel a little less breakable. Poe's lack of a proposed solution acted as a form of permission, an acknowledgement that the act of falling apart, of losing one's shit utterly and absolutely, wasn't a sin, or even a weakness, but a shared part of the human condition.

Charlie Waterfield stood up. He looked for Poe but couldn't see him. Poe was already back behind the wheel. Having found the radio station he was looking for, he looked up and, seeing that Charlie was still in the middle of the road, began honking loudly and repeatedly.

'Thank you,' Charlie said.

Charlie took several deep breaths. He looked up at the sky. He saw a tiny black dot falling through it. The black dot was too far away for Charlie to run after. He would never catch it before it landed. All he could do was keep his eyes on it as it fell to earth. But Charlie's heart never hit the ground. It landed with a sudden and deafening boom on the roof of the Tachycardia Tower.

21

THE THEORY OF GIANTS

Dishevelled, panicky, and out of breath, Charlie ran into the lobby of the Tachycardia Tower. The lobby was large and filled with people, but no one even noticed him. Dishevelled, panicky, and out of breath was how pretty much everyone entered the Tachycardia Tower. Charlie went shoulder-first through the crowd to the elevator. The Up button was already lit. Charlie pushed it several more times. He waited impatiently. His brain tried to make itself useful by reading the company directory, and Charlie noticed a company name that he recognized: Sarzanello Systems, with offices residing on the sixty-seventh floor.

Before arriving in Metaphoria, Charlie had never read or heard the word *Sarzanello*. He still didn't know what it meant. But this was the third time in less than thirty minutes he'd encountered it. This, Charlie surmised, must be metaphoric. The elevator arrived. Charlie got in. Thirteen other people did as well. He did not press the button for the ninety-ninth floor. He pressed the button for the sixty-seventh.

At the sixty-seventh floor, Charlie was the only one who got out. A red velvet carpet ran the length of the hallway. Crystal chandeliers hung from the ceiling. At the far end of the corridor stood a Giant. The Giant looked uncomfortable. His arms were crossed and he was hunched over to prevent his head from scraping against the three-metre ceiling. He was dressed in a black tuxedo with a bright red bow tie, which, judging from the way he kept pulling on his sleeves and adjusting his pants, were not the clothes he would have picked out for himself.

'I have an appointment,' Charlie said.

The Giant bent down to tie his shoe. Charlie, thinking he was safe, failed to pay attention, which is why he did not see the Giant pull a knife from his sock. The knife was long. The blade was serrated. The handle was pearl. Although it looked tiny in the Giant's hand, it was quite threatening when held against Charlie's throat. Charlie swallowed, which pushed his skin against the blade. A drop of blood slid down the edge of the knife and fell onto the carpet, where it left a heart-shaped stain.

'What were you before Metaphoria?' Charlie whispered. 'Director of Public Relations? CEO? Head of Acquisitions?'

'I ran a consulting firm that worked mainly with the federal government.'

'Advised world leaders? Pulled strings behind the scenes? Held the real reins of power?'

'All of those things.'

'You were a big man and now that you're forced to live here, in Metaphoria, they've reduced you to this. To being nothing more than a big man. That doesn't seem fair to me. Does it seem fair to you?'

'I didn't get it the worst.'

'You got it worse than me. And I was cog. An office drone. Did what I was told. People like you paid people like me to walk their dogs. Why don't you do something about it?'

The blade pressed a little harder against Charlie's throat. Charlie held his breath. The smallest amount of pressure was all it would take. And yet the Giant didn't push the knife forward. It's true that he didn't take the knife away, but he didn't add any more pressure either.

'What are you suggesting?'

'Walk away?'

'What would that do?'

'I have no idea. But you don't either. If you were to walk away from this, this moment, pressing this knife against this throat, Metaphoria would reward you. Or punish you. Who knows? Maybe you'll even poof! But what else can you do? Maybe I'm misguided, but it's hard for me to believe you're gonna trigger an epiphany while standing at the end of a hallway doing someone else's dirty work.'

Although imperceptible to anyone whose throat it wasn't held against it, the Giant reduced the pressure he applied with the knife. Then he puffed out a breath of air and turned his head slightly to the right.

'Whatever happens, you know as well as I do that if you drop the knife and leave this building, a whole new set of circumstances will open up for you. Maybe better. Maybe worse. But unlike this. If you change yourself, Metaphoria will change around you. You know I'm right.'

'I think …'

'What? What do you think?'

'I think that's true of back home too.'

'I agree.'

'It's just easier to see it here.'

The Giant continued to hold the knife against Charlie's throat. However, his eyes shifted focus. The knife fell to the carpet. The smell of burning cedar filled the air and the purple smoke was thick …

Poof!

22

THE CARDIAC OVERALL WRAPPING
AND RESERVE DEFENCE

When the purple smoke cleared, Charlie saw the elevator door that the Giant had been guarding. He pressed the Up button. The doors instantly opened and Charlie stepped inside. The walls were covered with mirrors. A military general in full uniform stood in the corner. He had six medals pinned to his chest. They were bright and shiny and attracted Charlie's attention. The General pressed the floor button – there was only one – and the elevator began to rise.

'What are those for?' Charlie asked.

'Avoidance.' The General pointed to the first medal. He pointed to the next five as he continued to speak. 'Repression, compartmentalization, denial, displacement, and suppression.

'Of the enemy?'

The General's furry eyebrows furrowed. The look he gave Charlie was a mixture of wonderment and sympathy.

'No, son: of love.'

'I don't understand.'

'Sounds like you've come to the right place, and just in time.'

The elevator stopped. The doors opened. The General had done nothing to make either of those things happen.

Charlie returned the General's nod and stepped into a large, open room that was blindingly white. The walls were white. The floor was white. The furniture was stainless steel. There were no plants. There was nothing in the space that wasn't man-made. Behind a desk made entirely of plastic and right angles sat Twiggy Miller. He wore a white lab coat. He and Charlie were the only two objects in the room that were, or even had been, alive.

'Mr. Yossarian?' Twiggy asked.

'Uh, yes?' Charlie answered.

'You've arrived a bit early.' Twiggy's voice was much deeper than the voice he'd used onstage at the Kummerspeck Theatre. His appearance had changed as well. He still wore a lab coat, but the sleeves on this one had been tailored so that only the tips of his finger-twigs were revealed. His hair was carefully combed and parted at the side. His body language expressed a calm professionalism. As Twiggy used the tip of his index twig to remove a speck of dirt from the pristine surface of his desk, Charlie wondered how much of this current persona was just as manufactured as the one he'd used to showcase the Spero Machine.

'My apologies. I tend to be a little too punctual.'

'Well, punctuality means on time.'

'My apologies.'

'So, how can we help you today?' Twiggy asked.

'I was hoping you could tell me.'

'Oh. Sorry. Are you ... are you not here for the procedure? The guard should have – '

'Of course I am.'

'Who's your reference?'

'I was told it would be inappropriate to say.'

'Very good!' Twiggy walked around the desk and shook Charlie's hand. His fingers didn't feel like Charlie imagined they would. They were warm and smooth. His grip was gentle. Twiggy stomped his right foot three times. The wall behind him lifted, revealing a secret room designed in the style of a log cabin. A deer-antler chandelier hung from the ceiling. The heads of moose and stags were mounted on the walls. In the centre of the room stood a stone fireplace. Two leather club chairs were angled toward the roaring fire. Twiggy led Charlie to the chairs, filled two heavy glass tumblers with whisky, and handed him a glass.

'To the human heart!' Twiggy raised his glass, and Charlie did the same. 'I know this is our first consultation, but I find it best to just jump right in. So let me ask you a personal question. How long have you been in Metaphoria?'

'Longer than I care to admit.'

'You see? Even that answer tells me so much. You're not proud to be here. Why? Because you've been told not to be proud. We've all been told that Metaphoria is, if not a prison exactly, some sort of re-education centre, summer school for the emotionally challenged. Would you agree?'

'Something like that, for sure.'

'Let me tell you: the opposite is true! Metaphoria is a gift. It is a wonderland! The possibilities are endless.'

'You don't want to get home?'

'Never. And let me explain why. And let me do so using the very question we've all been told is our best means of escape: have you figured out what the function of the human heart is?'

'I'm still here, aren't I?'

'Then it's not too late for you! In the Old World, the answer is so clear. The purpose of the human heart is to push ten pints of blood around a hundred miles of veins and arteries. The idea that the heart is the source of love was just metaphoric, something to jot down on a Valentine's Day card. But here, in Metaphoria, the human heart really is the source of love. And this is where the curse of Metaphoria becomes a blessing. I have learned how to use Metaphoria to my advantage, and I can do the same for you!'

Charlie held out his glass. Twiggy refilled it. Taking a long sip, Charlie leaned back in his chair.

'No longer a muscle, a rudimentary pump, in Metaphoria the human heart truly does generate and transmit emotion. Chief among them is love. Let's take it deeper. Because the question isn't 'What is the function of the human heart?' It's 'What is the purpose of the human heart?' So, in order to fully answer that question, let us ask ourselves about this substance the heart spends so much of its time generating. What is the purpose of love? It isn't rainbows and hugs, let me assure you of that. The common conception of love is ludicrous in its inaccuracy. Love is a thing with teeth that takes what it wants. Do you agree?'

'Truly.'

'Think of all the things you've done for love! Think of all the horrible, selfish, cutthroat, downright evil things you've done to keep love, to acquire more of it. '

'I agree completely!'

'Now, add to that list all the ways love has made you hurt yourself. Think of all the decisions you would have made differently, the goals you would not have struggled to attain, the energy and time and effort you would not have devoted to hopeless, improbable causes if you hadn't been doing them for love. Love doesn't serve you: you serve it.

'But no more! Let us be rid of love forever. We have found a way to prevent love from ever becoming your master again. We have figured out how to make the human heart impervious to love.'

'How?' Charlie was surprised by how quickly this word came out of his mouth.

'We have created a system.'

'The Spero Machine?'

'I'm glad you've brought that up. And I feel like I can trust you enough to admit that the Spero Machine is an unfortunate but necessary lie. You've seen a performance?'

'I have.'

'I'll say it straight: the Spero Machine is designed to extract hope. That's what those performances are for. We don't tell people if their love is true – even in Metaphoria no machine could do that. Rather, we collect their hope and then, using a patented process that utilizes darkness, a confined space, and a large amount of stress, we burn off impurities like realistic expectations and self-respect.'

'Realistic expectations and self-respect are impurities?'

'We turn regular hope into this: Hope #108.' Twiggy pulled a clear glass vial from the pocket of his lab coat. Inside was a glowing orange liquid. Opening the vial, Twiggy poured a drop of it on the tip of Charlie's finger.

'Go ahead. Taste it.'

Charlie did. It tasted like oranges on the cusp of going bad.

'Hope #108 is so pure that when applied to the human heart it stops all the love you generate from going out and all the love from outside that's trying to come in. And that's basically what we offer here: we take your heart and dip it in Hope #108, which hardens into a coating that surrounds your heart, making you impervious to love. Love is an addiction. We are here to help you kick the habit.'

'I …' Charlie began, and then he stopped. He checked his watch. It looked like this:

0 HR 23 MIN 16 SEC

Charlie did not attempt to repress or deny that he only had twenty-three minutes before the bomb, which sat where his heart should have been, exploded. It seemed like there were so many things he should spend those last twenty-three minutes doing: calling his kids, finding Wanda, sitting still and pondering whether the sum of his decisions had amounted to anything. But, if he were honest with himself, which the limited time he had left on the planet ensured he was, what he wanted to do more than anything else was to undergo the procedure and learn what it was like to be impervious to love.

'Can we do it immediately?' Charlie asked.

'We can do it right now.'

'There's one problem. My heart has been cut out and is currently on the roof of this building. In my chest is a bomb that's set to go off in … '

Charlie looked at his wrist.

0 HR 23 MIN 9 SEC

'Twenty-three minutes!'

'Twenty minutes is more than enough time. The fact that your heart is already removed will quicken the procedure.'

'And the bomb isn't a problem?'

'Don't you worry about that bomb. We can save you from the bomb. We've handled worse. You go get your heart. I'll scrub up.' As Twiggy stood, the west wall of the lodge lifted, revealing an operating room where several nurses prepared a brightly lit, sterile environment.

'You've had ... Have you had the procedure?'

'I was patient zero.'

'Good to know.'

'Just before you go, I am legally obligated to make you aware that our procedure, patented as the Cardiac Overall Wrapping and Reserve Defence, is irreversible. Once performed, you'll be free of the need for love, but you'll never feel it or express it ever again.'

Charlie thought about all the pain and suffering love had made him feel. He couldn't remember the last time love had made him happy. It did not take him long to make his decision.

'That sounds ideal,' Charlie Waterfield replied. He struggled to hold back his tears. Whether these tears were prompted by relief or remorse was something even Charlie didn't know for sure.

23

SWITCHING CHANNELS

Charlie was in the main elevator, ascending to the roof of the Tachycardia Tower, when the Unnamed Ghost suddenly reappeared. Charlie did his best to ignore him. He looked at the elevator buttons. He looked at the floor. He pretended to read the advertising bolted to the walls. But no matter where Charlie looked, the Unnamed Ghost hovered into his view.

'You're making a grave mistake,' the Unnamed Ghost said.

'Who are you?'

'I can't tell you that.'

'Why? Why can't you tell me this?'

'It's not the way these things are done.'

'So you can tell me, you've just chosen not to.'

'That's ... true.'

'Then what good are you?'

'I'm a manifestation of your innermost turmoil!'

'Are you? I guess maybe you are. But honestly, what use is that? How does that help me? I am so sick and tired of all of the goddamn self-improvement in this town! All this striving to be better, these outrageous efforts to become a better person. What if I'm okay with who I am? Where's the harm in that? Name me one thing in nature that isn't broken. Point out a single tree that doesn't have a broken limb, a river that doesn't flood, anything that won't be wiped away by water plus time. There's nothing! Absolutely nothing! Being broken is the natural state of nature!'

'You're just having a bad day.'

'No. Don't do that. Don't negate what I feel because you don't like it.'

'I'm not negating anything.'

'How about this? How about you fuck off?'

'What? You're telling me to fuck off?'

'I am!'

'Fine!'

The Unnamed Ghost disappeared. The elevator continued to rise. The other twelve people in the elevator, none of whom had seen the Ghost, put as much space between Charlie and themselves as the condensed space of the elevator allowed. Sixteen floors from the top of the Tachycardia Tower, Charlie took the walkie-talkie out of his pocket. He set the channel to Linda (Ex-Wife). He pressed the Call button. As her phone started ringing, Charlie steeled his courage. It came as a significant relief when the call went to voice mail. Charlie waited for the beep.

'I think, what's been so hard for me, so difficult for me to deal with, to admit, is not that I still love you, but that I've stopped. How can that be? How can something so life-changing and significant as love, a dollop of the divine falling into our everyday lives, disappear? How could I have been so careless? And that, more than anything else, explains why it's been so difficult for me to let go of all this. To admit that I've let something so unique and rare slip through my fingers, a Ming vase fumbled to linoleum. But it's okay. I've found a solution. Neither myself, nor anyone else, will be plagued by love, either toward me or from me, ever again.'

Charlie put the walkie-talkie away. He was the only one on the elevator when it reached the ninety-ninth floor. He still hadn't called Wanda. The doors opened. He got out. The walkie-talkie was still in his hand. He saw the sign pointing to roof access. He switched the channel button to Wanda. He spent several moments in the hallway staring at the walkie-talkie, although he did not use it. Charlie realized he didn't have the strength to tell Wanda the truth about what he was planning. He decided to just be okay with this. He knew that having that conversation would be so much easier after he'd had the procedure. He knew she had the power to talk him out of it. Charlie turned off the walkie-talkie and put it back in his pocket, which is why the Cardiac Overall Wrapping and Reserve Defence has the acronym it does.

24.

THE ROOF OF THE
TACHYCARDIA TOWER

Charlie stood on the roof the Tachycardia Tower, looking west, one hundred storeys above Metaphoria. He counted six people flying. There was clearly a sea monster in the harbour. He found it hard to take his eyes from the flaming tall ship sailing down the main street. The primary geographic feature of the north end was a mountain, with roads and houses wrapped around it and an incredibly vulvic cave entrance on the south side. As one would expect, there was a tall phallic tower, complete with slight curve, rising above the south. There were so many wonders that Charlie couldn't look away, which is why he didn't notice the path of the Cyclops's fist until it connected, with grace and intention, with his left eye.

It was not the hardest punch the Cyclops had ever given him: Charlie rose upward, but not that far. As he fell back down, the Cyclops caught him. Holding Charlie by the lapels of his purple velvet jacket, the Cyclops walked to the edge of the Tachycardia Tower and dangled him over.

'Wanda left me this morning. Did she tell you?'

'I haven't heard from her.' Charlie resisted looking down. 'I thought she was trying to fight the zombie clones of her old boyfriend.'

'Are you surprised that she left me?'

'Fuck you,' Charlie Waterfield said.

The Cyclops was not so impressed.

'Fuck me?' The Cyclops shook Charlie vigorously. These efforts had the opposite effect of what the Cyclops intended: the more the Cyclops shook Charlie, the more Charlie laughed.

'What do you want me to say?' Charlie asked. 'I didn't know you were with her when we met. Obviously, I either ignored or suppressed the signs that she was married. I will admit that. But doesn't the fact that she slept with me say something? Doesn't the fact that she fell in love with me say even more? Come on! Where's your self-respect? Where's your self-preservation? Where are your standards? Why do you want to be with a woman who doesn't want to be with you?'

'She does want to be with me.'

'Not for the right reasons.'

The Cyclops started shaking Charlie even harder. His body flopped around like he'd been deboned. His head bounced in unpredictable ways. His right shoe came off. Charlie and the Cyclops watched it fall. The ticking grew louder as the shoe got smaller. At the sixty-seventh floor, the shoe was so small they couldn't see it anymore. The same was not true for the ticking, which remained loud in Charlie's ears. Inspired by the poetics of the falling shoe, Charlie had an epiphany. He waited to smell burning cedar and see purple smoke. Neither of these things arrived, so he decided to share the epiphany with the Cyclops.

'The failure isn't when love ends. It's refusing to accept that it's gone.'

'You'd like to believe that, wouldn't you?'

'I know it to be true.'

'Wouldn't that be nice if it were. It would make everything so easy.'

'Accepting that love is gone is no easy task.'

'That's because you're a coward. And that gives me comfort,' the Cyclops said. 'To know that you will never be brave enough to love Wanda Parks. Not fully. Not with passion. Every day you will have to live with this. Every day you will be forced to confront the truth that a woman as wonderful as Wanda Parks has fallen in love with you, but you are too fearful to love her back. You will pretend that you love her with all your heart, but your heart is cowardly. Eventually, you will begin to realize that that's why she stays with you. That this is the real reason she fell in love with you in the first place, why she continues to love you: because you're unavailable to her.'

The Cyclops fell silent. He looked Charlie in the eyes as his grip began to loosen.

'This is going to hurt you very much. And it still won't be as much pain as the pain you've caused in me.'

'What about your revenge? I'll never learn that Wanda only loves me because I can't commit to her emotionally if I'm dead!'

'Oh, Mr. Waterfield. Have you really not figured out how this place works?'

'Wait! Wait! Do you still love her?'

The Cyclops stared at Charlie, or rather in Charlie's direction. The Cyclops's eye was focused on something invisible and far away. When the Cyclops did look back at Charlie, he had clearly forgotten all about him and was surprised to find someone dangling at the end of his fists.

With great power and little care, the Cyclops tossed Charlie away.

Charlie rose upward. He was three storeys above the roof of the Tachycardia Tower when the Unnamed Ghost appeared beside him.

'Hey, asshole! Pay attention! What are you doing?'

'I'm ... What am I supposed to be doing?'

'He's got it, Charlie! That Cyclops has figured it out! You guys are stuck on the same thing! Why do you think he keeps showing up? And he's done it! You're missing a chance to free both of us!'

The Unnamed Ghost disappeared. It was at this moment that Charlie realized his name: he was the Ghost of Charlie's Capacity to Love. Charlie looked down as he continued going upward. He saw the Cyclops sit on the roof, put his chin in his hands, then rub his eyes. The Cyclops was crying. He issued a deep, forgiving laugh. It was unclear who the Cyclops was forgiving.

'Charlie! It's so easy! You should do it too.'

'Do what? Do what?' Charlie asked.

But Charlie's question arrived too late. Even though he continued rising upward at an alarming rate, so that he was now the highest object in all of Metaphoria, Charlie could see the purple smoke gathering around the Cyclops as he sat on the roof of the Tachycardia Tower ...

Poof!

25

NAKED AND TINY

The purple smoke cleared as Charlie fell toward the roof of the Tachycardia Tower. The speed of his descent was rapid. Charlie took deep breaths. His palms started sweating. His heart beat faster, although Charlie couldn't see that because he was so high above the Tachycardia Tower. His left shoe came off. His watch slipped from his wrist. His pants, jacket, and shirt fluttered away. Charlie looked down and saw something directly below him on the roof. It was his heart. His superior vena cava pointed up like a smokestack and Charlie fell through it.

Sunlight shone through the walls of Charlie's heart. The farther he fell, the less light there was. He landed on his tricuspid valve in near total darkness. He looked up at his right atrium, which was cavernous. Charlie experienced a serene calm, which stopped his shrinking, although he remained tiny. And then, suddenly, the tricuspid valve opened and Charlie fell into the total darkness of his right ventricle.

The moment Charlie began to believe he would never stop falling, he landed in a thick, tarlike liquid. The impact didn't produce a splash, although it did provoke the liquid to emit a bright orange light, like phosphorescence in the ocean. The glowing orange tar clung to his arms and legs, making it difficult to swim. He could not touch the bottom.

Struggling, he swam to the ventricle wall and tried pulling himself out, but he couldn't. There was nothing for his feet to step on. The walls of his ventricle were smooth and slippery, and Charlie sunk below the surface of the tar.

As Charlie struggled to regain the surface, he swallowed some of the glowing orange tar. It tasted like Hope #108. He struggled to swim through the tar but soon became exhausted. Unable to resist, he sank to the bottom of his heart.

As Charlie waited to run out of breath, he pieced together what had happened. His divorce, or rather his inability to get over it, had caused his heart to produce an overabundance of hope. This excess hope clogged his left ventricle, a dark, confined space. Add the stress of the divorce, and Charlie's heart became a natural environment for the distillation of pure hope, which had coated the inside of his heart, making it impervious to love.

Discovering this explained a lot to Charlie. It also left him with a decision: either he eliminate the hope of getting back together with his wife, or he drown in it. And even though Charlie understood the choice in these terms, it took him several moments before he decided to get rid of it.

With the last of his strength, Charlie swam to the ventricle wall. He raised his bare foot. He kicked downward. Nothing happened. He did it again. He kicked three more times. On the fourth, a little bit of sunlight came in. The amount of sunlight, while small, weakened the pure hope just a little bit. Charlie continued kicking. His kicks became more effective. Soon the crack got larger. It grew in length and width. More light flooded into his ventricle. The crack became a hole and the hope streamed out of Charlie's heart, carrying Charlie along with it.

26

THE EXACT LOCATION OF
TWIGGY MILLER'S HEART

Charlie Waterfield lay on his back on the roof of the
Tachycardia Tower. The sun burned away the sticky
orange hope stuck to his body. Small pebbles dug into his
skin, but Charlie remained perfectly still. He closed his
eyes. When no purple smoke or smell of burning cedar
arrived, Charlie sighed heavily, stood up, and brushed off
the small stones that were stuck to his skin.

'Always gotta be the hard way with you,' Charlie said to
himself.

The first thing Charlie found was his watch. He strapped
it on. He was naked except for the watch, which looked quite
odd, but nobody else saw. Charlie closed his eyes. He took a
deep breath. He let it out and looked down at his wrist.

O HR 17 MIN 28 SEC

This did not seem like enough time. Charlie scrambled
to collect his clothes and his heart. He dressed, stuffed his
heart back into the breast pocket of his jacket, and ran to
the elevator.

The elevator doors opened as he approached them. It
started descending as soon as Charlie was inside it. The
button for the first floor was already lit. No one got on for
a hundred floors. The doors opened, and Charlie stepped

into the lobby. The shoulder-to-shoulder crowd of well-dressed, busy-looking people parted, forming an aisle that allowed Charlie to run to the payphones. As Charlie approached, the phone in the middle started ringing. Charlie, nearing the end of his first full day in Metaphoria, picked up the receiver without hesitation.

'Shirley?'

'Do you have Twiggy's heart?'

'How quickly can you get to my office?'

'Fifteen minutes?'

'You'll have to do it in ten and you're going to have to convince Twiggy to meet us there. He won't come if I try to bring him.'

'Not a problem.'

Charlie ran out of the Tachycardia Tower and was trying to hail a cab when he noticed that his apple-red Corvette was parked at the curb, directly in front of him. The engine was running. The driver's-side door was unlocked. The Cyclops's ring was no longer chained behind it. Charlie put his heart in the passenger seat, fastened the seat belt around it, and pulled into northbound traffic. He drove very quickly. He caught every light. His car suddenly had lights and a siren. Traffic in front of him pulled over to let him pass. There was a parking spot in front of his building. Charlie collected his heart and ran up to the office of the Epiphany Detective Agency. Shirley and Twiggy were waiting.

'You do not have much time.' Shirley plucked Charlie's heart from the breast pocket of his jacket. She put it in the middle of Charlie's desk. Together, they watched it beat.

'This isn't Twiggy's!'

'It's mine.'

'You told me you had it!'

'I can tell you where it is! It's right there!' Charlie pointed to Twiggy's chest.

Twiggy tried to bolt through the door of the Epiphany Detective Agency. He was very quick. The twigs of his right hand had already grasped the doorknob before Shirley had time to take off her gloves and snap her fingers, which froze Twiggy completely. She undid the buttons on Twiggy's shirt. She put her ear to his chest. She closed her eyes and sighed out her disappointment.

'I don't hear it, Charlie.'

'It's encased in hope. A special industrial kind of hope. Hope #108. That's what Twiggy was developing with Kitty. Together they found a way to make the heart impervious to love.'

'Convince me.'

'The Spero Machine? You know about that? It doesn't tell people if their love is true. It was never designed to do that. It's a hope-collection unit. Twiggy needs massive amounts of normal hope to make Hope #108. He used himself as a lab rat. Maybe Kitty too? I don't know. But that's why you were so sure Twiggy had lost his heart. It's encased with Hope #108. He can no longer send or receive love. But it's in there! His heart's in there, Shirley!'

'Is this true?' Shirley asked Twiggy.

'You can get it too. It's a very simple procedure. It makes you stronger than love!'

Shirley put her hand lightly against Twiggy's cheek. Twiggy remained frozen. It was unclear whether he would have reciprocated this gesture or not. Shirley kept her eyes on the eyes of her husband.

'You know who deserves to be treated better than this? I do.' The expression on Shirley's face wasn't anger but a sort of wonder, as if she were astonished to discover that something she'd always thought difficult was in fact quite simple. 'You don't treat me very well. Maybe you're a good person, but you're not a good person to me. That's what it's for. Jesus, Twiggy — that it! The purpose of the human heart isn't to make me strong enough to keep loving you. It's to prevent me from ever ending up with someone like you in the first place!'

Shirley became still. She looked up at Charlie, but her eyes were focused on something very far away …

Poof!

27

THE CONSEQUENCES OF
THE C.O.W.A.R.D.

The smell of burning cedar and the clouds of purple smoke cleared from Charlie Waterfield's office, but the ticking in his ears remained. He looked at Twiggy, who in Shirley's absence had come unfrozen. Twiggy patted down his hair. He straightened his tie and tucked his dress shirt into his dress pants. But nothing Twiggy did fixed his dishevelled appearance. He looked a mess because he was one. He opened the office door, but stopped when he was halfway out.

'I wish I could feel sad about this,' Twiggy said.

'You don't?'

'I've just lost the love of my life.'

'There are very few things harder.'

'But I don't feel anything about it! Nothing! Shirley was the greatest love I've ever known. And I don't feel sad or destroyed or even upset! This absence of emotion is the worst feeling I've ever had!'

Twiggy looked across the room at Charlie. His eyes didn't focus on Charlie. They focused on something very far behind him ...

Poof!

28

00:00:17

Charlie was alone in the office of the Epiphany Detective Agency. He closed his eyes. The ticking grew louder with each tick. He could not resist looking at his wristwatch. He had seventeen seconds left. He didn't know what the purpose of the human heart was. He could repeat all the answers everyone else had given him, but he knew that none of them were true for him. In the absence of anything else, hoping that it might trigger inspiration, Charlie opened the only window in the Epiphany Detective Office and stuck out his head.

'Love ends. I understand that now. Some loves last a short time and some a long time, but all love ends. Also, I now know that a love that ends doesn't negate its authenticity. That there is no connection. A love that ends was still love. But still, surely love, like any other organic thing, can be tended. It can be nurtured and soothed and given what it needs to grow and thrive. So if it does have a tendency to vanish as mysteriously as it appears, surely there must be someone to blame. No? Am I just wrong about this? Who can explain this to me?'

The people on the sidewalk and those looking out from the windows of all the buildings fell silent. Not a single person said a word. They waited for Charlie to answer his own question, this being a common thing in Metaphoria.

Knowing it was now or never, Charlie closed his eyes. He had faith that his epiphany would come.

It didn't. The ticking in his ears got louder and louder and then the bomb in Charlie's chest went like this:

t

h

r **BOOM!**

e

a

29

HOW THINGS WORK AROUND HERE

Charlie was just as surprised to wake up as he was to see Wanda. Seeing himself reflected in the lenses of Wanda's glasses was disturbing: his shirt was torn open, his chest stitched together with imprecision and haste, his left eye was swollen shut, both of his lips were split, and three of his teeth were missing. Charlie was in very rough shape, but also extremely happy to still be alive. The absence of the ticking was so absolute he didn't notice it. When he did, Charlie sat up quickly, causing the stitches in his chest to dig into his skin.

'I'm alive?'

'Of course you are, Charlie.'

'But the bomb? It went off … '

'That's what bombs do.'

'Why aren't I dead?'

'Oh, Charlie. Haven't you figured out how things work here yet? They don't let you die in Metaphoria. You just get beaten up until you finally figure it out.'

'Is it back?'

'What?'

'My heart.'

'Do you want me to check?'

'Would you?'

Wanda put her ear against Charlie's chest. She heard it beating.

'It's in there.' Wanda kept her ear pressed against Charlie's chest. She listened to Charlie's heart. She noticed that it beat in a series of long and short beats, which she recognized as Morse code. She listened carefully and discovered that Charlie's heartbeat was repeating the same three-word sentence.

"♥♥ … ♥♥♥♥ / ♥♥♥ / ♥♥♥♥ / ♥ … ♥♥♥♥ / ♥♥♥ / ♥♥♥,' Charlie's heart beat, again and again, and Wanda couldn't hold back her tears.

'Did you defeat the zombies and save the world?'

'I did. Will you stand up?'

With some effort, Charlie stood. Wanda wrapped her arms around him. She felt the muscles on his back. She felt his chest push into hers. Charlie held her tightly. Several moments passed before he realized the significance of this. He turned his head and pressed it again her chest and listened to her heart. It beat a series of long and short beats. If Charlie had known Morse code, he would have known that her heart was spelling out *I love you too.*

'Charlie, do you know what this means?' Wanda ended the embrace. She held both of his hands tightly. Charlie looked her in the eyes. He saw them shift focus.

'No. Not yet.'

'You feel that?'

'Please? Not yet.'

'You're no longer emotionally unavailable to me, Charlie! And yet I still love you! I can feel it, from right in my heart, that I still love you!'

'Please don't leave me.'

'I think I love you even more than I did this morning!'

Charlie hugged Wanda. He did this so he could stop seeing how her eyes were focused on something very far away. Charlie closed his eyes so he wouldn't see the purple smoke, but there wasn't anything he could do about the smell of burning cedar...

Poof!

THE PURPOSE

Leaving the keys in the ignition and the door open, Charlie abandoned his car and walked inside the Prison of Optional Incarceration Necessary to Terminate or Lower Excessive Shame and Self-Reproach. The sound of his shoes echoed down the empty hallways. Charlie did not slacken this pace until he came to the cell he'd formerly occupied. The door opened for him. It slammed closed as he stepped inside. The cot creaked as he sat down.

Leaning forward, Charlie put his forearms on his legs. He bowed his head. Although he tried staring at something invisible on the floor in front of him, his eyes wouldn't stop focusing on the small stains in the concrete. Charlie looked to his left. He noticed a prisoner with a long white beard in the cell directly across from his. The prisoner's cell was decorated with fresh flowers and thick books and charts of the sea. It was clear that he'd been in there a long time and that he planned on being in there for decades to come.

'There's always hope, right?' the prisoner said.

'Hope is a useless thing.'

'Oh, you don't believe that.' The Ghost of Charlie's Capacity to Love materialized in Charlie's cell. He no longer wore the orange chains. He looked much happier. He floated to the cot and sat down beside him.

'I don't have much time,' the Ghost of Charlie's Capacity to Love said. This was true. The Ghost had become very transparent and his transparency increased with every second that passed.

'So let me ask you this, Charlie: are you guilty?'

'Of what?'

'Of fucking up your marriage.'

Charlie shut his eyes. He concentrated on the last days of his marriage. Without being filtered by the vast amount of hope that had built up in his heart, Charlie saw all the things that he had done wrong. He saw the arguments that could have easily been avoided, the things he fought for that he didn't really want, the housework he didn't do, and the concessions he didn't make.

'There was someone to blame. And that someone is me.' Charlie's eyes remained closed.

'What are you going to do about it?'

Charlie opened his eyes and discovered he could see something very far away. He refocused his gaze. He realized that what he was seeing was the back seat of a Nissan Rouge, very late at night. It was at this point that he began smelling burning cedar. His cell filled up with purple smoke. Charlie searched his heart. Inside it he found the power to forgive himself.

And he realized that this had been its purpose all along.

Poof!

THE HEART'S MORSE CODE

A ♥❤
B ❤♥♥♥
C ❤♥❤♥
D ❤♥♥
E ♥
F ♥♥❤♥
G ❤❤♥
H ♥♥♥♥
I ♥♥
J ♥❤❤❤
K ❤♥❤
L ♥❤♥♥
M ❤❤
N ❤♥
O ❤❤❤
P ♥❤❤♥
Q ❤❤♥❤
R ♥❤♥
S ♥♥♥
T ❤
U ♥♥❤
V ♥♥♥❤
W ♥❤❤
X ❤♥♥❤
Y ❤♥❤❤
Z ❤❤♥♥

Andrew Kaufman lives and writes in Toronto. He is the author of international bestseller *All My Friends Are Super-heroes*, *The Waterproof Bible*, ReLit Award–winner *The Tiny Wife*, and *Born Weird*, which was named a Best Book of the Year by the *Globe and Mail* and was shortlisted for the Leacock Award for humour.

The author wishes to thank Mom, Dad, Liz, Marlo, Carl, Michele, Zach, Andy, Phoenix, Frida, and the ultimate kick-assedness of Alana Wilcox.

Typeset in Walbaum.

Printed at the Coach House on bpNichol Lane in Toronto, Ontario, on Zephyr Antique Laid paper, which was manufactured, acid-free, in Saint-Jérôme, Quebec, from second-growth forests. This book was printed with vegetable-based ink on a 1973 Heidelberg KORD offset litho press. Its pages were folded on a Baumfolder, gathered by hand, bound on a Sulby Auto-Minabinda, and trimmed on a Polar single-knife cutter.

Edited and designed by Alana Wilcox
Cover by Ingrid Paulson
Author photo by Karri North

Coach House Books
80 bpNichol Lane
Toronto ON M5s 3J4
Canada

416 979 2217
800 367 6360

mail@chbooks.com
www.chbooks.com